MW00877662

Hunting Trip

Hidden Blood Book 3

Get new release notifications first via the Newsletter at

PLEASE RETURN TO LIBRARY REH

Men

"Put it through that bit there," I said helpfully.

"Huh?" snapped Faz. "Put what through where?" He glared at me, sweating like a yeti in a hot spring during a heatwave. Served him right for wearing his suit. He even had his jacket on, the utter muppet.

"Put the longest pole through the guide at the top."

Faz scowled then threw the tent pole down in disgust. "That's it, I give up. There's obviously been a mix up. They gave us the wrong bits or something." He stormed off and the whole sorry mess of a half-erected tent collapsed.

"Hey, what's happening? Let me out, let me out." Mithnite punched at the tent from inside where he'd been holding it up so Faz could assemble it easier.

The comedy act had been going on for forty-five minutes now, and what was funny at first become a lesson in just how impractical in some regards my husband was.

Faz walked back to the tent and raised an arm, his shoulders hunched up by his ears in anger.

"Don't even think about it," I warned.

"What?"

"You were gonna blast it, weren't you?" I glared at him but couldn't stop myself smiling.

"Um, maybe a little. Stupid bloody tent. Why couldn't we go glamping, hire a yurt or something?"

"Because this is fun, that's why. Grab a chair and sit down. You need a rest."

Faz gave the mess of material and poles a final look then ambled over and took one of the new fold-up chairs identical to mine. He snapped it open, plonked himself down, then promptly toppled sideways as it folded in on itself.

I stared down at my dear husband on the scorched brown grass, raised an eyebrow, and said, "Seriously? You can't even open a chair?"

"Bloody camping shop sold us a load of duff equipment."

"Hold the baby, I'll do it." I passed him Kane, and Faz's face lit up as it always did when he held our son, then stood up and went to sort out the chaos.

Ten minutes later the spacious tent was assembled, Mithnite was safely extracted, and the baby was fast asleep. Faz may not have excelled at camping but he was a whiz with the little one. What took me hours, he did in minutes. I'm sure they had a pact and did it to wind me up.

Persimmon and Dancer joined us from their swanky tent, more like a generously proportioned house judging by the size. One of those multiple room versions for large families, complete with bedrooms and a separate cooking area. I kept my smile on my face even though I was jealous, but in a nice way.

"You had to help too?" asked Persimmon, frowning at Dancer who was as sweaty as Faz.

"Yup. You'd think the Head of all things magical and his number one enforcer could put up a tent."

"Men," sighed Persimmon.

"Men," I agreed.

"Hey, we are here, you know?" said Dancer, wiping his forehead with a crisp white handkerchief.

"We know," we both chorused.

"But you could have worn more appropriate clothes." I suggested. "What's with the suits?" Faz wore a smart nineteen-sixties affair complete with white shirt and black tie, Dancer's a more modern cut, but again, white shirt, and a much narrower tie.

With his usually slicked back hair, although presently it was rather unruly, he looked like an undertaker, not the man in charge of running the various magical creatures of the UK. Faz's hair was freshly dyed blond, and he was gaining weight for the first time in almost a year. He was, finally, recovering from an ordeal that had left him almost dead and ended up with me inheriting Hidden magic he himself had been gifted.

So here we were, a bunch of magical misfits, a vampire, her wizard enforcer husband, our boss and friend, his shifter girlfriend, our lodger-cum-family member, Mithnite, and our baby, now eight months old and a constant source of worry.

Hardly surprising when I'd gone from pregnant to giving birth all in the space of ten days. That would freak out any mother.

That's magic for you, it never ceases to surprise.

"What we doing first?" asked Mithnite, stripping down to his vest and jeans like a sensible person.

"Ooh, look at those muscles," said Persimmon with a twinkle in her eye.

"Hey, don't be cheeky." Mithnite let his long hair fall in front of his face to hide his embarrassment, a habit I was sure he'd grow out of as he advanced through his twenties.

"I don't think she was," said Faz, studying his body like the rest of us.

"You look buff, dude."

"You think?" Mithnite flexed and muscle rippled. He was lean, but his chest was broad and his shoulders wide, with slender arms bulging in all the right places.

"Yeah, what's the secret?" asked Dancer, who'd always been like Faz, slim and sinewy because the magical furnace burned bright. Boy did it take a lot to fuel them.

It's a definite boon to having magic. I got my figure back quickly after giving birth, but I guess the short pregnancy helped with that. Although, my damn breasts were still like balloons, not that I got any complaints from hubby about that.

"Been working out," said Mithnite, trying to act nonchalant but smiling like a loon.

"We should have a session together some time," said Persimmon with a wink.

Mithnite blushed but grinned back at her, and no surprise why. Persimmon's own vest clung to her dark skin like plastic wrap, revealing breasts larger than even mine, her perfect figure the envy of every woman she'd ever met.

"Enough of this, let's eat," said Faz, who's appetite was insatiable now he was recovering.

"I'll get wood." This was the perfect excuse to do some preliminary exploring, and truth be told I couldn't wait for some alone time. So I kissed Kane, fussed about making sure he had everything he needed, then wandered from the clearing in the nice spot we'd found and went in search of firewood.

As I entered the forest, the birdsong grew louder, the coolness calmed my skin, same as the trip was already doing to my slightly jangly nerves, and I wondered if life got better than this. After so much turmoil the last year it was just what we needed. Life had been turned on its head once we had a child, zero sleep, magical mayhem around every corner—nothing new there—and Faz had even returned to do a few very easy jobs. I'd had my hands full so was off the books as an enforcer for now, and to be honest I missed it.

Being a mum is great, best thing in the world, but when your days are usually filled with bashing wayward wizards or supernatural creatures over the head or blasting them with magic, changing diapers and having your adorable baby clamped to your breast like a limpet for half the day, and the other half is taken up with washing or trying to catch a few minutes of sleep, feels very odd indeed. It's a hard thing to admit, but I missed the action.

It took minutes to gather firewood. The crazy warm summer had dried everything out, and after eking it out a little longer, I wandered back to camp with my arms full and my spirits soaring. This was going to be a great week, just what everyone needed. No magic, no phone calls in the middle of the night, just a chance for me to take it easy while Faz and Mithnite looked after the baby. They'd promised I could have some me time, could go off on my own for long walks, and generally be spoiled.

It was going to be awesome.

"Right, let's get this fire going and cook like we're cavemen," I said with a huge grin as I dumped the wood down by the circle of stones I assumed Persimmon had made as it looked quite professionally done.

No answer.

I turned, but there was nobody there. Frowning, I checked our tent but it was empty.

"Not funny, guys. Come on, Kane needs feeding. Faz, this is not clever."

Still nothing. I checked Dancer and Persimmon's tent, but it was empty too.

Surely they wouldn't have gone off without me? I scanned the area but saw nothing. Just trees, the cars, the tents, and the track we'd driven down. We were in the heart of Snowdonia, miles from home, but there were lots of paths leading in all directions as the whole area was a designated camping ground. Vast swathes of land where you could camp for free as long as you cleaned up after yourself.

Maybe they'd gone for a walk? But all their stuff was here, all the baby things, and Faz was utterly paranoid about taking the changing bags with him. He didn't go anywhere without a dozen nappies, three changes of clothes, and more wet wipes than was practical for even the most extreme of emergencies.

I spun hard on my heels at the sound of Kane crying. I ran to our tent, pushed aside the flap, and dashed inside. I pulled back a sleeping bag and there, wriggling and smiling, was my baby. Picking him up, I clutched him tight, and got a very bad feeling.

There was no way on earth Faz would leave his son alone even for a minute. He slept in our room, he went with us everywhere, Faz would never go off and leave him like this.

"Guess the holiday's over," I sighed, and I swear I didn't mean to, that I was worried and scared and all that, but a little smile spread across my face, just for a moment.

Game on.

Some Detective Work

Familiar feelings surfaced as ink tingled and magic came to life like a bear prodded from hibernation with a big, sharp stick. It surged and eddied like it had been waiting for this to happen. I guess it had. I guess I had.

So many months had passed where I'd hardly used magic at all. My focus was on the baby and I didn't have the energy. From the moment I discovered I was pregnant, I was consumed with worry. Worried the baby would be born a monster, the rapid gestation resulting in something too terrible for a mother to stand. But he was perfect in every way, grew at the usual rate once born, cried and screamed and suckled and smiled his gorgeous smile, just like a normal baby.

But part of me longed for the rush of violence, for magic to flare and my body to dance under the power of the Empty. The anticipation turned instantly to dread and shame. What was wrong with me? How could I, even for a split second, want something bad to happen? What kind of person did that make me? I cuddled Kane tight and he fell asleep, unconcerned by whatever had happened.

I understood something then. That it wasn't so much me wanting bad stuff to happen, but the magic inside needing a release. And the moment I believed something was amiss, it took its chance and sent an insane amount of chemical combinations coursing through my veins, confusing my body and mind.

It's why some people smile at funerals. They are so close to crying, to breaking down and weeping, that the signals get mixed and they laugh or grin instead. You feel awful, how could you do such a thing? But it's just your body acting up in times of deep stress.

Fun most definitely over, I left the tent and turned slowly in a circle, listening with enhanced senses, searching the trails and the woods for any heat signatures. Nothing.

We were alone.

Getting my act together, I cradled Kane as I checked the tents and cars thoroughly, just in case I was missing something. I wasn't.

Everyone's things were still here. Nobody had taken anything they didn't already have on their person. Faz had his suit, same as Dancer. Mithnite and Persimmon, the buff ones, were down to trousers and vests, and everything else was exactly as they'd left it.

There was no sign of a struggle; I'd heard nothing from in the woods. They were just gone.

I settled down on the chair and nursed Kane when he woke and began to nuzzle for a feed, all the while waiting for something to happen. But it didn't, and after I changed the baby he dozed. I couldn't put him down though, was too afraid, too worried something might happen. So I held him tight and sat on a cheap chair in the middle of the woods, alone and frightened as the afternoon sun beat down and my imagination grew increasingly wild.

It wasn't like there was any shortage of people who'd want to see us dead. We all had enemies. Enforcers, Heads, shifters, demonic junior wizards in human form, vampires with Hidden magic, we weren't exactly enemy free, but that was the point. We were dangerous people. You didn't get to sneak up and carry us off without a fight. It just couldn't happen.

Except it had.

Working Solo

Why would anyone kidnap them? And how? Both questions had no easy answers. Killing them, missing out on getting me by luck, I could understand. But just take them away? No way would they go without a fight, and it would be one helluva fight too. You simply didn't get to grab people like my husband and friends without there being a major bloodbath. Probably several.

Or maybe it wasn't coincidence I was left out of it. Maybe it was a kidnap, however it was done. I wasn't sure who knew, although I assumed hardly anyone, but we had over a million in gold stashed away, Mithnite too, after the dwarves paid up, sort of, because Faz did a job for them. Was that what this was all about? Was I supposed to wait for a ransom note?

Haha, stupid. You didn't hold wizards, shifters, and Council Heads to ransom, you'd get your eyes popped out and your blood boiled for your trouble. Revenge then? It had to be. What other explanation was there? Someone, or multiple someones, had snatched them somehow. Surely there would be a sign of a struggle? I put Kane in the front carrier so he was wrapped tight against my chest and did a little investigating. The ground was clear, just the signs of us having set up camp. No scuffed ground, no magical residue, nothing.

I went to our car to grab my phone but remembered there was no signal here, part of the appeal, and found Faz's. Glancing in Dancer's car I could see his and Persimmon's too, so that was a dead end.

Venturing away from camp, I checked out the beginnings of the various trails but there were no dropped pebbles leading the way, no scraps of cloth tied to bushes, no nicks in trees, or broken branches, nothing to indicate anyone had been past recently. It was a large area with a lot of space for hikers so the chance of anyone being here was remote, and I could see no footprints because the ground was too solid.

I had a genuine mystery on my hands, and I did not like it one bit.

We'd had enough grief the last year to last a lifetime and then some. We'd only just got paid out on the insurance, and that was only after I insisted the insurance guy meet me in person. They changed their minds then and paid up, a bit of glamoring from yours truly helping speed things along. Our new place was nice but it didn't feel like home yet as everything was too new, too impersonal, so this break was just what was needed to escape reminders of the attack on our home and the destruction of so many good memories in the only place I had felt truly safe.

We were getting our life back together slowly, though, and we had each other, Kane, and friends, but the escape was overdue. The Chemist took his role as godfather very seriously and was constantly bringing gifts and fussing about, and as much as he was a great help when we needed to rest, it all became a little too much, too overbearing. Combine that with Grandma, who's dictionary doesn't contain the word interfering, it somehow having been replaced with "helping out," so when Faz suggested a camping trip I jumped at the idea.

Should have stayed at home and locked the doors instead.

Thwarted, I sat on the grass and moped. The baby slept, I tried to think, and the day grew warmer. I must have remained like that for fifteen minutes, sure I should be doing something, but not knowing what.

Everything changes with a child. I couldn't just go running around doing the vampire shimmer souffle as it would freak him out. I also couldn't let the violence erupt, couldn't charge headlong into any situation, as if he got hurt I'd never forgive myself. I was shackled, unable to be who I usually was when things like this arose—yeah, more often than you'd think.

So I stood up, got my stuff together, and drove away.

A Babysitter

As soon as the signal came back, I pulled over and made a call. I left Kane in the baby seat asleep, then got out and leaned against the car. Less than a minute later, the sun disappeared and a large shadow swept across the ground.

I smiled, knowing my friend had come through for me.

The dragon known as Delilah, a woman brave enough to open up a cafe-cum-deli next to the formidable Madge, she of the infamous fry-up, landed with grace beside the road. She shifted back into human form and sighed with pleasure. Her skin shone pale and perfect against the struggling grass, highlighting her rich auburn hair and green eyes. She was beautiful, slender and waif-like, but also more than capable, and willing, of frying you to a crisp when in dragon form. She is my friend.

"That was quick," I said with a smile as we hugged.

"I would have been faster but I got attacked by pigeons." She smiled, her wide eyes twinkling, and laughed with her head back, revealing a slender, pale neck. I'm never quite sure when she's joking or not. Pigeons? Delilah unhitched her backpack and dressed in a simple outfit of a white summer dress with a rose print. She looked divine.

"You sure you don't mind? It's a lot to ask. I would call Grandma but she's out of town on some witch business or other."

"Kate, it's fine. I'll look after Kane. I'll drive back in your car, you said you have Dancer's?"

"Yup, it's still at the campsite. Come on, I'll fill you in on the way." We got in and I drove back to the clearing.

Once there, Delilah did exactly as I had done. She studied the area, followed the trails, but found no clues. She shifted, searched from above, but returned ten minutes later with nothing to report. There was no sign of them, no hint of anything untoward at all. By now I was thoroughly creeped out.

"What do you think happened?" she asked, showing real concern.

"I have absolutely no idea. Something bad. Something really bad."

"You'll find them. You want some help? I can get in touch with anyone you want."

"No, but thanks. Until I know what this is, it's best kept between us I think."

We chatted for a while longer, then I showed her all the baby things, gave her some formula and explained about Kane's routine, and after another hug and then a big kiss for Kane, they were gone.

I don't know if I've ever felt more lonely than I did then. My husband was missing, so were my friends, my baby was gone, and I only knew for sure that one of them was safe. No harm would come to Kane, dragons are excellent babysitters. As for the others, I'd have to find out.

I rummaged through the bags I'd removed from my car, changed clothes from jeans and blouse to leather trousers, white t-shirt, hiking boots, and a rucksack with phone, keys, wallet, water, food, a few more necessities, and hitched it onto my back.

Just about ready, I heard a crash in the forest and was instantly alert. My eyes snapped to black, my ink swelled beneath my clothes, writhing like fat worms under the skin, and my incisors snicked down hard and sharp, already dripping the vampire's tear, the milky venom that can turn you or kill you. I never turn, but I sure as hell do kill.

I grabbed a coil of rope from the back of Dancer's black SUV, but also accidentally pulled the vinyl cord that lifted the lid on the compartment that kept all the tools for vehicle repairs, like he'd ever use them. Except it wasn't full of car jacks and a spare tire, it was a veritable arsenal.

"That's a bloody machine gun," I whispered, astonished.

I heard the sound of splintering wood, like trees were toppling, and lost my grip on the cord. The compartment slammed shut and I turned as a tree crashed into the clearing.

Out from the woods emerged the largest troll I'd ever seen in my life. I'd heard the mountain ones were a breed apart to the townies, but I wasn't expecting the difference to be quite so huge.

Dude was freaking massive.

Follow That Troll

A machine gun wouldn't help me, what I needed was a bloody big hammer and chisel and for him to lie down while I hacked away. The troll brushed aside the last few trees like they were blades of grass. Thick trunks snapped under his strength, splintering as he stepped forward into the clearing.

He stopped for a moment, took in the scene with typical glacial slowness, head turning on bunched neck muscles, traps so large they came right up to his ears, then he grunted and strode forward.

The stupid brute trampled the tents without pause, glanced my way once then turned back to face where he was heading, and marched with purpose, sweeping aside the trees with a single, lazy swipe. His arms were thicker than the tree trunks, his legs like ancient gnarled oaks, each finger bigger than my arm. He was easily twelve feet tall, shoulders just as wide, making him appear like a box of granite with old tree roots having grown over it, except he was all rock, maybe some mineral and quartz and the like.

He turned and stared at me as he entered the forest and I called, "Wait. Hey, where you going? Have you seen…" He was gone.

I thought about going back to the car and grabbing the weapons, but he was already getting away. Then I smacked myself upside the head, did the shimmer shuffle, and was loaded down with illegal weaponry in less than a second. The troll was easy enough to follow by sound and the trail of destruction he left behind.

Trolls didn't do this sort of thing, they had to be circumspect, and they usually stuck to the high, rocky areas where they couldn't make such an obvious scene. They may be Hidden and they may be veiled from Regulars, but it's hard to hide it when you swat trees like they're fragile plants. It makes things complicated.

This was far from normal, meaning, it was right up my street. With no other clues, or idea what else to do, I followed. This couldn't be coincidence. It had to be tied to the disappearances.

Aware that there could be others in the vicinity, I adjusted my gear as I went. I now had my own stuff, including several blades, the machine gun, plus two revolvers. They were shiny and heavy, and I liked them a lot. We don't get to have guns in the UK, they're harder to find than a friendly goblin, and strictly off-limits anyway for all Hidden. If the Council find you with one it's instant execution, no questions asked. Still, it was worth the risk, and besides, they were Dancer's so I was sure he'd help me out if anyone decided to tell. I stashed what I could in the pockets of my jacket, already sweltering and having second thoughts about wearing it, and slung the machine gun over my shoulder and covered it with a thin blanket.

Last thing I wanted was a walker to see, as even with a veil Regulars sometimes glimpsed enough to do something foolish before I faded from memory.

I paused. What was with the self doubt? I was a powerful magic user, a bloody vampire to boot, and I could amp up my veil without a problem. Why was I being so circumspect? It wasn't like me, especially since I got the Hidden magic. Lack of use? The caution that comes with having a child? I didn't have time for that nonsense.

I readjusted everything, stowed the blanket, kept the machine gun slung over my shoulder but ready at a moment's notice, and let the veil strengthen enough to make me entirely forgettable to any Regulars. It felt comforting having the guns, especially something large like this. The cold metal boosted my confidence as no matter how much magic you have, there's still something very satisfying about knowing you have a serious piece of weaponry at your disposal.

And I'd actually used something similar before, bizarrely on a holiday where you could hire all kinds of crazy weapons to shoot at things. It felt like a different life, but I remembered what to do.

I sped up to catch the troll but he was one fast guy and was causing absolute mayhem. Trees were either knocked over or large branches snapped off to block the way, meaning I couldn't just turn into vamp mode and dash after him as I'd get flattened. So I kept within the realms of normal human speed and remained alert to falling trees and unfamiliar faces as I trailed him through the woods.

It was less than five minutes before we exited and hit the true mountain. It was dry and dusty here, the landscape changed dramatically. From lush trees and cool air, we emerged into a world of rock. After a short walk across a flat expanse, the mountain reared up steeply, dark ravines below where sunlight seldom found its way.

Shale and fissures had captured many an unwary, unprepared hiker here, and every year the rescue services had to come get those who'd taken to the steeper parts without suitable equipment or sense, let alone food and water. You didn't need ropes and carabiners, any of that, it was just steep and easy to place a foot wrong and break something. So I trod carefully, kept well back from the troll, and thus easily dodged debris that tumbled behind him as he climbed ever higher like a monkey up a familiar tree.

This was the first time I'd seen a troll in its natural habitat. I was so used to seeing them in an urban environment that I forgot that this was where they belonged, where they were truly at home. They originated in Finland like so many supernatural creatures, so the rumors went. Something happened and they awoke, their quartz brains activated fully and they got enough sense to think for themselves.

With their newfound sentience, they decided to explore, and gradually, over the many millennia that followed, they came down from the mountains and their caves and mixed with other Hidden. They are secretive and not much is known about their old ways, as they aren't big talkers, but they have been here since the beginning of time and will remain long after humanity has expired. They watch, they record, the communal experience of millions of the creatures stored in each crystal brain, a living—sort of—record of the entire history of the planet. Boy would that make for some interesting TV shows if anyone ever found a way to tap directly into their minds.

But, let's face is, they're also as dumb as, well, as a big lump of rock in many ways, and they aren't keen on sharing their thoughts or being very friendly. This one was no exception.

Bored of dodging boulders, and wondering if the hike would ever end, I caught up with him, hoping we could have a chat now he felt more at home.

"Hey, hey!" I tugged at the big guy's arm and he looked down on me like he had an annoying gnat on his wrist.

"What puny human child want?"

"I'm not a child, I'm a grown woman."

"If say so. Go away." He pulled his arm away and began to move off again.

"Wait. I want to talk. It's important." I ran and grabbed him again but I must have overstepped the bounds of personal space as a frown formed slowly on his face as he turned. He looked down at me, upper lip turning up in a snarl. Trust me, on a troll it was seriously scary.

Before I knew it, he grabbed me around the waist, lifted me up, and threw me. He just chucked me like I was a stick, and the only saving grace was that he threw me aside rather than down.

Then I hit a large outcrop of rock and my back snapped. I didn't feel quite so lucky any more.

A Slight Problem

Vampires, by their very nature, are robust creatures. We break bones, snap our shit up, and it heals. Sometimes, I've felt my broken bones slot back into place and fuse so fast it was hard to believe anything was wrong. I've also had severe injuries that took hours to repair. The more serious the damage, the more intricate and slow the healing process is.

This was definitely not going to be a quickie.

I lay there on the jagged rock, numb from the waist down, unsure if it was a blessing I couldn't feel, or a curse, and wondered if this was how I would die. Alone up a mountain with my husband who knew where and my baby far away. Not a nice way to die, especially the alone bit. Would I heal? Could I come back from something like this? Hyperventilating, and with magic surging and adrenaline coursing through my veins, I was close to freaking out. My back was broken, I just didn't know where or how badly. What the hell was wrong with that troll?

Knowing it would smart, I gripped sharp rock hard with my outstretched hand and pulled. I screamed so loud it echoed around the mountain, scaring birds and scattering them to the sky, but I slid sideways and rolled down to a flat piece of ground, landing on my side. Once I'd gone from sweating to freezing to freaking and back again a few times, I discovered the pressure had eased. Still unable to feel my legs, let alone move them, I took a few shallow breaths to calm myself then took stock of the internal damage.

Several vertebrae were definitely broken, the discs had ruptured, the cushioning liquid spilling out, but the spinal cord wasn't ruined. If it was severed, then it probably would have been the end of the line, as there are limits even for vampires, but as far as I could tell the nerves were merely trapped because I was so out of alignment. If the magic flowed well then I should be able to recover. The only issue being, this was no straightforward repair where bones pop back into place and fuse in minutes, this was delicate work and my body knew it.

It was as though my inner magical workings were reticent to even begin repairs, as if anything went wrong I would never move my legs again. I focused, gritted my teeth, and shunted magic through the ink, felt it swirl and converge on my lower back where it eddied and spiraled through my tattoos, burning like pins and needles times a thousand.

I was soaked with sweat now, in utter agony as my splintered bones carefully and slowly reconfigured.

Shards split my skin then retreated, only to pierce my flesh in another place as fragments of bone sought their true resting place, moving this way and that, searching for their home in a way that wouldn't cause more damage.

My back rasped like grinding spices in a pestle and mortar, or maybe it was just my teeth. Each tiny shift of my body sent agony through my system, and I must have spent the next hour screaming, lost to the world. The only thing I knew was pain.

The afternoon passed in a haze of hurt, humiliation, and sweat. Fierce sun burned my pale skin, my leather trousers and jacket taunted me, telling me I was a fool for wearing such garb. I laughed at their jibes, for how much worse would this have been if I'd worn a nice dress and flip-flops?

Tiny birds grew brave and hopped about in front of me, cocking their heads and staring then squawking and flying away. The rock grew hot, my body so drenched in sweat it became a living nightmare. I passed in and out of consciousness repeatedly, and each time I jolted awake I tried to reach the backpack and get water, but dared not move my body for fear of ruining the work already done.

The day turned cool, and my body temperature dropped. At first it was welcome, like a dip in a deep lake after sunbathing, but as marrow grew and bone shifted, the cold began to eat at me just as the heat had. My fuel reserves were non-existent now, so the magic turned to fat and muscle stores to continue the repairs. It felt like I was eating myself from the inside out.

How much longer would this last? How much more could I take? How could I get an ice cream?

Click Clack

The freshness of evening turned to freezing night. Part of me welcomed the sun's absence, the bitter moon and the emptiness. My true home. The void called in the frigid air, whispered through the trees and taunted as the moon peeked from behind twisted clouds, confirming that one day this would be the summation of my entire existence. Nothingness. But before that, there would come a time when I would cry for, crave, search to embrace the night and shun the day.

Same as always, I would fight it, but it called nonetheless, drew out the vampire nature. The rock was colder than a wizard's toes—don't ask me why, but they're always like ice cubes—but even as I shivered, a fire raged within. I had a fever, brought on by shock and the explosion of chemicals as the internal damage was repaired.

On and on it went, me shivering then sweating, hallucinating about Faz walking past and ignoring me, about my baby screaming for his mummy and me stuck on this damn mountain unable to move for fear of doing more damage and never being able to play with Kane in the park.

Bats skittered past, darting low, using their sonar to hunt their prey. Oh, how hungry I was, how I longed to feed and feel warm blood spurt into the back of my throat. To swallow, feel the blood magic course through my veins and speed up this repair.

I'd been lax with feeding; having Kane had the opposite effect to what I'd expected. I'd been told I would be hungrier than ever, would have to feed regularly to provide sufficient milk, and although I had crossed more people off the list than usual, I had been increasingly sickened by the whole sordid affair. I'd brought life into the world, and the thought of taking it, even of despicable men who's acts of barbarism and cruelty were unimaginable, became anathema. Even they'd been babies once.

For my sins, I fed, but it made me ill and shamed. When I sat feeding Kane, knowing the milk he took was tainted with the blood of a human being, I came close to breaking down on many occasions. He was healthy though, thrived and grew at a steady rate, and praise the gods, he didn't have fangs or try to bite me or start doing magic or anything untoward. Just a regular kid, fed by his far from Regular mother.

Something snapped in my spine and I screamed in agony then was still. It was as though a dam had burst and everything sped up until I grew dizzy. Fire surged in my back, the muscles spasmed, adrenaline hit like a bullet train, and my ink engorged until I was fit to burst. Magic swirled and converged in spurts of primordial force that threatened to split me wide open, and then like a tsunami it retreated, sucked away and left me gasping for air and clawing at the rock.

I rolled down the escarpment and only stopped when I hit the base of a stunted, gnarled tree, as broken as my body had been. But there was no pain.

Gingerly, I moved my arms, then my toes, then my legs. I was whole, and I felt like a million dollars. Sure, I stank, my teeth were chattering, and my lips were dry and my throat parched, my skin blistered, and my back was sore as hell, but I felt magnificent. I sat up carefully, leaned against the tree, and got the backpack free. I fumbled about with frozen fingers and gripped a bottle of water. The cap was tight and I couldn't feel it properly but I released it eventually and spent the next ten minutes sipping slowly before downing the contents once my throat was working again.

Next step was to stand. Gripping the tree, I got to my feet and found that although stiff I had full feeling and mobility. I rubbed at my thighs and arched my back, did a variety of exercises to get the blood flowing and to loosen up.

I was whole, back to being Kate. Perks of being a magic-wielding, kick-ass vampire. Also one of the main drawbacks, as who the hell gets this kind of grief when they go camping? Hell, we hadn't even had the chance to burn any sausages or snuggle up in our sleeping bags yet.

The next hour was spent eating, more stretching, and getting accustomed to the night. As my strength returned so my eyesight kicked in. The world became tinged with green, tiny animals glowing orange as I registered their heat signatures.

Time to go pay a troll a friendly visit.

Knock, Knock

I crawled around the mountainside gathering everything up, spent several minutes with the trusty wet wipes, slung the gun over my shoulder, followed the route the troll had taken with my eyes, marking every rock, every hidden hole, nook, and cranny, then wound my way up carefully in his direction.

After a steep climb, I came to a terrifying overhang that left me dangling by my fingers with a mighty drop beneath. No, I didn't look down. I hauled myself up and there I was, on a large ledge covered in the carcasses of animals and several mounds of chalk. This was definitely a traditional troll. The city dwellers gave up on eating goats a long time ago, although you could never get them to give up the chalk.

The cave mouth was wide and high. Dark too, really dark. My eyesight was good now, excellent in fact, but when it was truly pitch black I couldn't see too great, and the thought of plodding in with just a torch to light the way didn't instill me with confidence. Instead, I decided to wait until first light.

Much as I wanted to just go gung-ho and bash some rock skull, if for no other reason than he'd nearly killed me, I knew that wasn't sensible and wasn't liable to get me answers. He had to have something to do with everyone's disappearance, it was too much of a coincidence otherwise. Trolls didn't smash around the woods like that, however daft they were. They had a set of inbuilt rules that governed their behavior and the fact he'd gone marauding meant trouble was most definitely afoot.

I huddled into a dark crevice and pulled the blanket over me, waiting for dawn.

Some time later, I came to with a start, cold and cramped, hungry and thirsty. I drank and ate and then crawled cautiously from my hiding place.

I stretched my back and looked down from the ledge to the treetops below. We were high, and it was beautiful. As birds stirred and sang joyously to the morning, I turned to the east and was witness to the most beautiful sight I have ever seen apart from the face of Kane moments after he was born in Grandma's living room. The sun rose over distant mountains, red and fierce, the bringer of joy, warmth, and life to the world.

Most vampires can't stand this sight, it sends them screaming for the dark, blistering and burning. Those under a few centuries old can function in the day and handle the light, but it gnaws at them, unsettles them. I loved it, and promised myself I always would. I lifted my head and let it warm my face, burn away the terrors in my mind and the tingle of fear I refused to acknowledge.

Then, smiling and feeling light and determined, I turned away from this source of all life and marched to the cave's mouth.

Light penetrated deep within because of the angle of the sun, yet soon it would be too high and if I waited I'd lose the advantage, so I rapped on the rock, whispered, "Knock, knock," then strode in.

A Fumble in the Dark

The cave stank, ripe beyond belief. Bones littered the floor and piles of chalk and other strange dusts crowded against the dry walls. It was disorganized and messy with many of the mounds of minerals trampled, the colors bleeding into each other, and it only got worse the further I went.

Light faded as I got deeper, so I turned on the flashlight. Nothing to see, just bone, dust, and rock. See, this is the problem with trolls. If they're still then they're hard to find, as they are made of the same stuff as the homes they inhabit in the mountains, so my nerves jangled even though I don't really get nervous any more. Yeah, that's what I kept telling myself.

He could be anywhere, be right in front of me, or beside me reaching out a huge hand to crush my head. I kept turning this way and that, shining the light at strange shapes and weird protrusions that came alive in my imagination. But it was just rock, nothing more. Deeper I went, until it was pitch black. A deep rumble grew in intensity, practically shaking the walls of the expansive cavern.

I followed the sound, down wide curved corridors, around bends, through large vaulted rooms with pillars reaching into the darkness. I cursed my idiocy for waiting until dawn; fat lot of good it had done me.

The rumbling grew louder, vibrating my bones and teeth, pounding in my skull like a giant's drum. And then I tripped over and found myself staring right into the mouth of the troll. No prizes for guessing where the noise emanated. I was almost deafened by his snoring as his chalk-tinged breath blew the hair from my face and cooled the sweat on my brow. Carefully, I moved away and stood. I shone the light down the length of his body, taking in the size of him. Boy was he a large one, bigger than I'd believed, and beautiful in his own way.

Strange lines criss-crossed his body, azure and deepest vermilion. Crystals glinted in the torchlight, and all the while he snored peacefully.

"Wake up, you big lump," I shouted in his ear as I kicked at his body, getting nothing but a sore big toe for my efforts.

I tried again, really loud this time, and still nothing but a grunt as he rolled over and snored. Next I poked a finger up his nose, but it was like pushing a straw into a wide-brimmed cup. I rammed my fist in instead and shone the torch right at his closed eyes. A heavy lid scratched at an eyeball then lifted. Slowly, the eye turned and focused on me.

"Why child wake Big Rock?"

"Because I want to have a chat. And you owe me. You nearly killed me."

Big Rock sat up with the sound of a cheese grater against stone as he slid his backside a little to face me, still sitting. He was taller than me even on his hard ass. "You child thing from other day? One in way?"

"That was yesterday, and I told you, I'm a woman. You nearly killed me," I repeated.

"Ugh, Big Rock forget own strength." He stretched and yawned, his body cricked and cracked like an avalanche, and I stepped back before he crushed me as he repeatedly lifted his arms up and down. What the hell? It wasn't like he had to get his circulation going or anything.

"What were you doing, lumbering through the forest like that?" I asked, squinting at him, wishing I could see better.

"Coming home," he said, like it was obvious.

"Okay," I said, exasperated. "Where have you been? Why were you out where humans could see you acting like that? It isn't how you're supposed to behave."

Big Rock focused his full attention on me and frowned, the rock shifting on his face like it would smash his brow to dust. "Had to get away. Bad things happen on mountain. Big Rock want comfort of home. Thought little woman was going stop me, so pushed away. Sorry."

"Damn, now you're making me feel bad." I scratched my head in thought, wondering what could have made him scared or worried. Trolls didn't get scared, they hit things with their fists and then the trouble went away.

"Sorry." Big Rock got to his feet, and he really was massive. He could crush me like a grape and I'd never be able to stop him. I thought about running away but wanted answers, so asked again.

"What's been happening? Why were you scared?"

"Not scared," he grumbled angrily, bending to peer into my face.

I backed up and raised my hands. "Okay, sorry. Why were you, um, going home then? What happened? Have you seen my friends? Seen other people?"

"Oh, seen lots of people. Bad things use people. Take people. Do strange magic. Big Rock feel it bad, make head funny. Keeps moving, never know where safe, best stay here, out way. Eat chalk." He straightened, then his face kind of shifted, almost like he was looking hopeful. "You got goats?"

"No, not on me. Um, so what is this strange thing? Who's doing it? What are they making the people they take do?"

"Not take people. Just use people. Come back but are mean, act odd. Bad vibe, all wrong in head and walk funny. Ugh, tired now, must sleep. You go away." With that he crashed down to the floor, pulled his legs up to his chest, and began to snore.

I thought about waking him up again but decided there was no point pushing my luck, so beat a hasty retreat to the welcome sunny day outside this strange home within the mountainside.

Seriously

I staggered from the gloom, the light blinding me as the sun shone low but directly into my eyes. I couldn't see a thing.

The air whooshed as if split with something very sharp, and out of pure instinct I dodged to the side. The sound of steel against rock rang out, followed by a "Get 'er," and several grunts as mighty weapons were wielded, ready to do me harm. All I could think was it was a good job I'd got a sitter, this would not have gone well otherwise. Not that it was going great so far. Another whoosh signaled something coming down at my head. I dodged again, and as my hair whipped through the air I felt the blade sail past my ear. A lock of hair blew in front of my face. My anger rose.

I whirled, facing away from the sun, and snarled at three dwarves with axes raised, looking about as grim and hairy as dwarves can look, and that's very grim and very hairy.

"Chop 'er head off," ordered a particularly grumpy looking dwarf. Like all of them, he, maybe she, was wearing the distinctive leather garb under chain mail. Each wore a leather belt rammed with hammers and chisels and spare weapons, had so much hair it was hard to see much of their face, and reminded me of stunted trees grown thick and gnarly, the tops lopped off when they grew over four feet.

Their weapons were huge, great battle axes no Regular could hope to lift let alone yield, but their massive forearms coped easily as they readied to cleave me in two.

"Um, can we talk about this?"

"What's there to talk about? Right, lads, first one to get 'er head can have extra ale this eve."

Seems like that was incentive enough and all three of them roared then charged, swinging as they did so.

In no mood for their games and, frankly, feeling a little put upon and wondering if I'd stepped into a weird fairytale, I let magic surface and sped from one dwarf to the next, circling behind and snicking off a fistful of hair from each of their beards before they knew what was happening. Then I raced to the side where I'd slept that night and shouted, "Hey, over here," and held up their hair. My magic-infused fingernails shone bright and as sharp as their axes as the sun glinted off the keratin. I let the magic fade and with it the sharpness.

"Why, you…"

"Oi, where's my beard?" asked another as he ran a hand through his trimmed facial hair.

"That's… that's not right that ain't. My beard!"

All three were astonished, incensed, outraged, shamed, and a little worried. A dwarf's beard is sacred, a sign of their maturity and their very dwarfness, and they abhor anyone touching it, let alone cutting it.

"Right, you lot. If you don't play nice then I will shave all three of you bald, scalp you, then kick you back down whatever sorry excuse for a cave you came from. Plus, I'll tell everyone you lost to a girl. A human girl. So behave," I lectured. "Or else."

They were lost for words. They spluttered and they commented on each other's beards, and did a lot of glaring, then put their heads together and discussed matters in their own language, fast and furious and apparently with lots of arguing. A minute later they broke from their huddle and said, "Agreed."

"That's more like it. Now, what's this all about?"

Their spokesman strode forward confidently, and not to miss out, the other two did the same, each of them puffing out their chests and still clutching their axes so they didn't lose face in front of what, after all, was a mere human female. "We thought you was one of them."

"One of who?"

He shrugged his shoulders. "Dunno."

"Eh? Look, why were you trying to kill me? Who did you think I was? One of who?" I repeated.

"Like I said. Dunno. One of the… er. What's the word?"

"One of the crazies," said another dwarf.

"Yeah, one of the crazies. Thanks, Badden Moltenhammer."

"My pleasure, Aberthol Sandygravel."

"What crazies? What's going on here? First everyone gets kidnapped, then the troll in the cave tries to kill me, now you guys. What's this—"

"Oi, I'm not a guy," said a dwarf that looked about as feminine as a tree dressed in chain mail. Wielding an axe. With a beard. "What's wrong with you?"

"Yeah, don't go disrespectin' our womenfolk. "

"Sorry, my mistake. Can you please tell me what's happening?"

Something shifted then, and I saw the sly glances they cast each other as they closed in a little, thinking I hadn't noticed. They were trying to double-cross me, the sneaky buggers.

"Um, sure. Why don't you have a little sit down and we'll tell you all about it," said Aberthol.

"Oh, okay," I said, smiling sweetly.

Their shoulders relaxed a little and I took my opportunity.

With a surge of energy, I swept past them, and using bare strength I grabbed hold of two beards in one hand, one in the other, and yanked. I'd expected to get a handful of hair in each fist but instead the dwarves came along for the ride. Guess the hairs were in deep.

I dragged them over the rock to the edge of the escarpment, then with them wriggling and shouting and trying to get a good hack in with their axes, I stepped right up to the edge and dangled them into the void.

"Your choice," I said sweetly.

"Fine," said Aberthol with a sigh.

"Yes, we'll talk," said Badden.

"We'll talk," agreed the female.

"Good." Then I dropped two of them.

Feel my Wrath

As they screamed and plummeted, I threw the female back then whirled to face her. She stared in shock at the empty space, then her eyes turned to me, hiding her fear. Dwarves seem to have the insecure gene mostly missing, but she wasn't exactly brimming with confidence either.

"Bone Cruncher will destroy you," she shouted, then kissed the blade of her battle axe and charged.

Sometimes dwarves are stupidly gung-ho. I simply sidestepped. She swung at air, lost her balance, and screamed as she hurtled over the edge.

Now, you may think this was all rather callous of me, but have no fear, I'm not that bad a person, honest I'm not.

With a smile of sweet satisfaction, and then a frown because I was wasting time and still no closer to finding anyone or figuring out what on earth was happening in this godforsaken place, I walked to the edge. I lifted my arms to my side, let my coat flap dramatically, the wind tussle my hair, then leapt into the abyss.

The dwarves were waiting for me below, looking abashed on the ledge I'd encountered on my climb up but they'd obviously not known about. I knew there was something off about these guys, and the fact they weren't aware of the ledge confirmed it. What self-respecting dwarf wouldn't know the terrain like the blade of their axe?

I landed with one knee bent then stood and turned, glaring at them. All three had their heads down and looked sheepish. "Ugh, I've had it with you guys." I snapped the gun from my shoulder and pointed it at them.

They glanced around nervously but the ledge was only as wide as the three of them side by side. There was nowhere for them to go, nowhere to hide, nowhere to run.

"I want answers, and I want them now."

"Fine, we'll talk, but not 'ere," said Aberthol Sandygravel, eyes darting in all directions.

"Where then?" I asked, already sighing inside as I knew the answer. "Don't tell me, inside the mountain, right?"

"How'd you guess?" he asked brightly. "We've just opened up a new seam and one of the tunnels we excavated led here, but this place is spooky. The old gods ain't happy 'ere and we've already lost good men."

"Oi," said an indignant female.

"Er, and women. Sorry, Llyn Sulfurkiller. We was supposed to come check it out, but we've lost two dwarves already. Let's get out of this terrible place."

I was impressed. Dwarves aren't big on talking, and long sentences are not their forte, so this was serious. I decided to stick with them for now, maybe they'd have some clues as they sure didn't seem to have any answers.

"Fine. Which way?" I asked.

"Over there." Aberthol pointed in a vaguely northerly direction toward a range of mountains maybe an hour away, looking wistful, pining for the comfort of the world underground.

They weren't keen on staying out in the open like this. Even those that lived in cities preferred to spend most of their time underground. It's why they love the Hidden Club so much. It has cheap booze, there's a good chance of a fight, and it's in the basement. What dwarf could ask for more?

"After you," I said, so off we went.

Feeling Antsy

For seriously stocky dudes, dwarves are exceptional climbers. I had a hard time keeping up as they clambered over boulders, swung across chasms, hung from their fingers and dropped to dangerous rocks below, all just to shave a few seconds off the route when there were easier ways to go. They were like wild mountain goats, sure-footed and confident in their surroundings. But there was a definite edge. They constantly stopped to search the area, staring at suspect bushes and standing motionless to peer into the gloom of the patches of forest we passed, never once entering even if it would have allowed us to make better time.

And they refused to speak. Once in motion and focused on a goal, they shushed me whenever I spoke, and wouldn't answer questions. All would be revealed once we were somewhere safe, was all I got, and then they spoke no more.

The day grew warmer, I grew increasingly impatient, and the dwarves were almost skipping after an hour of hard hiking as we clambered up a steep hill and the heat radiated back so hot you could fry an egg on the bare rock.

"How much further?" I asked, sipping from my almost empty water bottle.

"Another hour or so," said Llyn.

"What!? You said it was only an hour to get there."

"If we went via the forests. But they ain't safe. There are things, eldritch things in there, that's how we lost our kin."

"Fine, but can we please hurry? I need to find my friends." I got the distinct feeling I was on a wild goose chase here. They didn't know anything, or nothing that could help me anyway. But there would be others, and they might have encountered something, or maybe these guys really did plan on spilling the beans once underground. What other choice did I have?

I stashed my water bottle in my rucksack resting on the ground and heard a grunt and the sound of tiny rocks tumbling down the slope. I turned to see the three dwarves apparently bouncing down the hill and into the woods, moving faster than anything I'd ever seen before. They were a blur and then they were gone.

"Damn," I muttered, then grabbed my gear and bolted after them.

Now, I'm fast, I mean as fast as a train, but there are limits. I can't outrun a speeding bullet or a jet fighter, and I couldn't keep up with the dwarves and whatever creatures were carrying them off.

I hit the woods and entered the cool dark interior. Up ahead, branches snapped as they passed, and as I sped forward I was repeatedly slapped by whip-like saplings that sprang back at me. I was so close, but I wasn't gaining, so I needed to keep up the pace and hope they slowed at some point. If not, then I just had to follow until they reached their destination, and hope it led to Faz and the others.

My speed increased until I was moving as fast as I dared through the dense woods. I couldn't go full-throttle, there were too many trees and things that could snag me or trip me up. I may be speedy but I could come a cropper same as if I moved slow, and although my senses were attuned to the environment it's different when you're moving rapidly. You can't take in the terrain the same way and accidents can happen.

But they were getting away, and with them my only clue. I powered-up, took a risk, and burned through the scant reserves of energy that were dwindling with each footstep.

I was gaining on them, so I slowed a little, thinking it best to hang back and wait until they got where they were going. This was it, I was going to get everyone back. I just had to hold my pace and everything would be fine.

It wasn't.

No End in Sight

On and on we went, passing from the empty forests and the deserted craggy hills to softer, more lush landscapes at the heart of hiking country. I heard hikers talking up in the hills where there were well-worn paths, and we skirted several campsites where children laughed and played and adults talked while they relaxed with beers or a sneaky Prosecco from a plastic cup.

Where were we going? What was this all about? My quarry was getting ahead of me as I focused on the people and upped my veil, fearing for their safety and everyone else's. Surely whoever was doing this wouldn't be taking them somewhere so close to Regulars? That made no sense at all.

Then I found the bodies.

Pause for Thought

The three dwarves lay dead, bodies sinking into deep moss at the heart of a swathe of forest. They looked almost peaceful, like they were sleeping on a soft, green, oversized mattress. Maybe having a doze before they headed off to split heads or bash rocks.

Or they would have, if not for the look of terror on their faces. I crouched, searching them for signs of violence, but they were unmarked as far as I could tell, and I wasn't about to go rummaging around under the leather and chain mail as who knew what I might find. No wounds, no obvious signs of bodily damage, just dead. Magic was thick in the air like a fog. Nasty magic. They'd been killed by something or someone powerful. It had been swift and without mercy, the only good thing about this. At least they hadn't suffered. But why kill them, and how?

The bodies turned cold and gray within seconds, and as I watched, the flesh, the clothes, even their weapons began to crumble like salt rubbed between your fingers. Soon there was nothing left but ashen stains on the verdant forest floor. They couldn't remain here, they were true Hidden, and as their spirits left to return underground to say a final farewell to their kind, so their bodies were absorbed by the earth and their essence taken back to the Hidden realm.

Then there was nothing, no sign they'd ever been here, and I wondered if the whole thing had been a figment of my imagination. Had they been real, or were they ghosts leading me somewhere, telling me which way to go? Were they nothing but the souls of dead dwarves wanting to help me in my quest?

Haha, so stupid. Of course they'd been real. Dwarves didn't go out of their way to help humans like this, it wasn't in their nature. They'd been alive all right, and now they were dead. Whoever had killed them was getting away.

Grim-faced, I got to my feet, finished the last of my water, munched on a handful of raisins, then let magic become my world. I ran for all I was worth, following the wisps of twisted energy that dissipated even as I chased through the forest, the signal weakening then vanishing like it had never been. Like I was alone in the world, running around Snowdonia in circles, dreaming of dwarves and trolls and death and kidnappings. Maybe I'd wake up in the tent and find I'd been having a nightmare.

Nope, this was a living nightmare and my family was gone.

I kept going, the trail having vanished now, just an inner something telling me I was on the right track, that this was the way they'd passed. But truth be told, it could have been the route any number of hikers had taken and I was going in entirely the wrong direction. I didn't think so, though. Intuition told me I was on their trail, that if I kept going I'd find them, so I forged ahead, resolute.

For an hour I ran, heading south, away from the heart of Snowdonia and its beautiful forests, lakes, and mountains, and I must have covered fifty miles at least. This was nuts. Surely I'd lost them, overlooked something? They wouldn't go this far, would they?

But I kept moving as fast as I could, now little more than a jog, all excess energy consumed, my body running on empty. I was winded, my side hurt, my heart ached, and my mind reeled, but I would not stop until I found them. Never.

With a summoning of power from deep within, I increased the pace slightly only to slam into something invisible. My head cracked, my nose split open, my lip spurted blood, I chipped a tooth, and even hurt my knee.

The last thing I thought before I bounced back and hit dirt was it was a good job I wasn't speeding.

Wasn't Expecting That

I opened my eyes and grumbled, lamenting a time when I never got knocked out by invisible forcefields and my face didn't get pulverized on quite such a regular basis. My nose re-calibrated, got the all clear, then did the fast grind back into place. My favorite lip, the pouty bottom one, flattened as it was engorged with new blood, my wonky knee shifted painfully as it searched for the sweet spot like a keen lover groping in the dark, then popped into position, and everything generally hurt like hell, but in a good way. Meaning, I'd lost no essential bits and pieces. Blood zinged on my tongue, and desire for the all-consuming high such delights from non-Kate sources brought clouded my mind. For a moment I was lost to lust.

But I snapped back to reality fast and hard as I was finally getting somewhere, was about to get answers.

Springing to my feet, I stared at, well, nothing. It was just more woods, same as it had been for ages. Trees and moss and nothing out of the ordinary at all.

Squinting, I could see there was something off, almost like it was a painting or photograph, and it took a while to understand what the problem was. Nothing moved. There were no leaves blowing gently, no heat haze, no birds, no gentle shifting of the forest as creatures burrowed or scampered. It was static.

I stretched out my fingers carefully toward the invisible barrier and felt its energy. This was strong stuff indeed, the best. Shaking my head, I lowered my arm and brushed myself down. Then I wandered away, wondering what to have for lunch and which way it was to the campsite.

After ten paces I pulled up short; something niggling at me. Hell, I'd almost forgotten all about this place, nearly gone about my merry way without giving it a second thought. This was no simple veil, no barrier to stop people from seeing what was on the other side, or from entering, this was doing much more.

Anyone passing wouldn't get close enough to touch it, would be repelled by the energy it contained. That would certainly be the case for Regulars. It was only because of my nature that I stood a chance of remaining where I was, but it pushed at my mind, trying to insinuate itself inside and send me away none the wiser or even caring.

I turned, and stepped forward cautiously with my hands held out and came into contact with something as solid as a brick wall. It was truly a thing of wonder, but there was a darkness to it. This wasn't formed by a benign magic user, this was conjured by somebody with strength but with a definite edge to them too.

Evil. Cold.

It was frightening. This was power, real power, but I kept my hands in place and sought to delve deeper.

I was no expert, far from it, but you can read magic to a degree, get a basic understanding of how it's been made and its function, even the intent. This was a multi-faceted veil, magic made real, and had been willed into existence not by one but several. Combined forces used to create something that would last and keep those inside safe and hidden. Made from dangerous magic, drawn from the Empty and warped to become something anathema to most practitioners.

The energy messed with your mind and that was not something Hidden permitted. There were Laws, and the Council took a very dim view of anyone who used their knowledge to interfere with another's private, intimate thoughts. Imagine if everyone was allowed to meddle with other people's personalities, their memories and emotions? Yes, exactly like vampires.

We only got away with it as it was used for feeding, not to manipulate the flow of the Regular world. Any vampire caught screwing about in the heads of Regulars or Hidden to influence them beyond the most simplistic and short term actions would be summarily made very, very dead. Didn't stop a lot of vamps pushing the limits, but limits there were.

So who would be doing this? Certainly strong Hidden, but human or something else?

Like I needed to ask. It's always humans. Always.

Since I'd become embroiled in this Hidden world, I'd learned a thing or two, and one of those was that veils are illusions. Sure, they are real in one sense, but they rely on the bending of natural forces, a warping of the laws of physics and also of the mind. It's as though you accept it even though you don't even know it's there, and if the mind takes it as the truth then so does the body. So I had to become a disbeliever.

There was no way I could negate this, but with the power I held I thought I could find a way through. Convinced it wasn't a good idea, I nonetheless had to see inside. This was where everyone was, I was sure, and whatever faced me I had to try. My family might be being killed right this moment for all I knew.

Buoyed by the thought of impending disaster, I let my body relax a little then focused on my magic. Ink fattened and magic swirled through the beautiful marks that covered my entire body. It meandered with grace through the chakras and increased in power as it did so. Awareness intensified as it gained focus through the power of my will, and as it mingled with the blood magic of the vampire my hands became almost translucent as I sought to become one with the veil, to vibrate on the same wavelength and become this energy.

I felt the change as an intense, not unpleasant tingling, then a thrumming as I pulsed to its strange rhythm. Like a light strobing fast then slow, fast then slow. In my mind, I pictured myself as a being of light, as solid as the mirage before me, then I closed my eyes and walked. It felt like passing through fire, every nerve set alight, and then nothing.

I was on the other side.

Standing before me like a dark messenger of death was a woman.

"Grandma?"

Overdid It

My body snapped back to my old self, a sudden sense of solidity that didn't match the lightheadedness I experienced as my brain struggled to process what I was seeing. This made no sense.

Was I hallucinating? Grandma couldn't be here, it wasn't possible. She was at a witch convention or something, wasn't she? What would she be doing here? How could she be involved in this?

It was like finding your cute puppy had just tortured the next door neighbor's cat and eaten it alive. It didn't compute.

She stood in a large clearing, immobile. The ground was mostly dust, with small tufts of stubborn grass dotted here and there. There was a huge fire pit deep with ash. Embers glowed hot in the middle, and around it were benches and logs to accommodate a large group of people. Another smaller fire pit was close to a covered area, a makeshift kitchen of sorts judging by the pans and piles of metal plates.

Dotted around, were small wooden huts that reminded me of something, but I couldn't quite recall what. Where had I seen them before? What was going on?

I'd walked into something I ought not to have walked into, disturbed something that didn't want to be disturbed, and I got the distinct feeling I wasn't welcome.

"Bugger off, Kate," said Grandma crossly.

See, told you.

The Good, the Bad, and the Grumpy

We stared at each other for an eternity. No wind blew, no sound came to my ears after Grandma's words, the only movement I focused on was her nostrils flaring as she breathed. I had all the time in the world to study her. This adorable old lady, thousands of years old and as kind and considerate as you could get, who gave the best hugs and made the best tea, who I'd never once seen not wearing her house coat and her pink fluffy slippers, whose hair was gray and brittle, whose thick tights were always slightly wrinkled, the traditional witch epitome of a harmless old lady, she didn't look like that now.

Grandma was… evil. And scary. And very witchy, in a "cackle while I eat your children" kind of way. Her usually hunched back was ramrod straight, making her look a foot taller, almost my height. Her hair was lustrous and sparkled with something oily mixed with what appeared to be ash. She wore all black, and not just any black, but garb so devoid of color it was akin to staring into the Empty itself. Her loose trousers and lightweight cloak, complete with requisite hood, hung off her solid frame, sucking in the light. She was an impossibly dense presence, powerful beyond belief, dominating the very earth she stood on and the space she inhabited in a way I couldn't quite understand.

Power. That's what it was. She oozed power. It emanated from her and she seemed to have no actual physical outline. She shimmered and morphed, black sparks of magic fizzed and popped and spat from her body and clothes, blurring the boundaries of the physical and meta until she became all there was, expanding to encompass the entire universe. And her features were off, the same yet different, making me uneasy and nauseous. More than anything, I wanted to run. But I couldn't, because however odd and freaky this all was, it was Grandma. But too much Grandma, like the essence of her wrapped up in power she'd never let manifest before. Definitely a "Cor blimey, guv'nor," moment.

I was mesmerized. She took up all my focus and attention and there was nothing left over for anything else.

"What… what's happening?" I croaked, my thoughts becoming my own, my mind and body beginning to function again.

"You shouldn't be here," scolded Grandma, somehow becoming more familiar, although it was still disconcerting seeing her wearing this hardcore magic user's outfit.

"I could say the same about you. Why on earth are you here?"

"Later, first a hug." Grandma came to me, as I somehow still couldn't bring myself to move, then wrapped her arms around me as deadly forces sparkled off her.

I tingled all over as she held me, then slowly I responded and the familiar feeling of protection, of love and warmth, and the smell of lavender and strange potions made me lightheaded as always and I knew this was still her, that underneath it was the same woman.

But it wasn't right, it was like Grandma distilled, like she was trying too hard. Maybe this was her true self finally revealed? It was a Grandma hug, but almost too much Grandma. Weird.

"That's good. That's great," I sighed. "Oh, Grandma, it's been terrible. Everyone's gone, a troll nearly killed me, then there were these dwarves and…" I released my hold and took a step back. "You were bringing them here, weren't you? Why did you kill them?"

"You foolish child. We didn't kill them, why would we? It was them, the others. They caught up to us and did them in. We were trying to save them, get you safe too, but you had to keep going, didn't you? I should have known, no family of mine ever gives up."

"I don't understand. What are you talking about?"

"I think we better have a chat, don't you, love? Fancy a cuppa?"

I realized I was parched, and as surreal as it was, I nodded vigorously and said, "A cuppa would be lovely. It's about the only thing that would make any sense about now."

Grandma smiled wickedly. "That's the spirit."

So we had a cup of tea.

Confusion Abounds

I tried to take in the clearing as we walked over to the oversized fire pit where a blackened kettle straight out of a western was bubbling away hanging from a tripod. I counted ten small huts, assembled hastily from random lumber and several cut boards, and I realized where I recognized them from. Witches often lived together in compounds, forming groups so they could earn a living running one business or another, and used these simple designs for their sleeping quarters. Usually with several bunking up together for warmth and to gossip the night away.

But there were no other witches, nobody else I could see. The only sign of any others were a few pieces of clothing hanging from makeshift washing lines and oversized trunks beside the huts. It made absolutely no sense at all.

We were silent as Grandma delved into a plastic tub and pulled out metal mugs and even a few biscuits. She served us both and then we sat on logs opposite each other, and drank and ate. I was famished and could have eaten the whole packet, but I had to get answers first. I wasn't sure where to start.

Grandma understood my unease so after we'd finished she broke the silence. "I assume you haven't found them?"

"What? No, of course not. Look, not to be rude or anything, but will you please explain what's happening? Why are you here? Why are you dressed like that? And how do you know they're missing? Did you know it would happen?"

Grandma tutted, she's an expert tutter. Got her tut down to a fine art. She gives lessons to other witches. "I know they were missing because I'm a witch. I'm Grandma. I'm dressed like this because this is a serious business. Actually, it's fun," she said brightening. "Been years since I got all dressed up and went into full witch mode."

"Grandma! What's happening?" I was frustrated beyond belief. So exhausted I could have slept for a week. And confused, very confused.

"Sorry. Let me explain."

"Please."

A familiar scent wafted past, bringing with it memories of a full stomach and rude behavior. I searched for the source, and saw someone crouched over at the smaller, more organized cooking area. This was getting too much, I must be dreaming, surely? "Madge? Grandma, is that Madge?"

The figure turned and waved, in a grumpy way. It was Madge all right. This just got weirder by the minute.

"It is. We came to sort this mess out once and for all."

"Ugh, I think I'm going to throw up or faint or something."

Madge wandered over and I followed her with my eyes, too stunned to do anything else. My stomach grumbled. "Here you go. I even brought you cutlery."

In her familiar fashion, Madge practically slung the steaming plate of food at my lap. I caught it and stared from her to the fry-up and back again, not knowing whether to tuck in or throw it away just because I was angry.

"What is happening?" I shouted.

"Eat up, then we'll tell you everything," said Madge, looking to Grandma who nodded in agreement.

So, feeling utterly discombobulated, I ate a fry-up in a clearing protected by a veil, while Madge and Grandma looked on and my husband and friends were out there somewhere, in who knew what kind of danger.

Some days are just peculiar.

An Explanation

I finished my food and placed the plate beside me. The two women stared at me intently.

"What?" I asked, beginning to feel uncomfortable.

"Um, love, would you mind putting the machine gun down? They're dangerous, you know," said Grandma in her most calming voice.

I glanced down, only to realize it had slipped off my shoulder who knew when, and I'd been almost cradling it in the crook of my arm, probably the whole time. It was pointed at them. "Oh, oops. Sorry." I rested it on the ground carefully then said, "Okay, spill it."

"There's a problem," said Madge.

"You're telling me," I said.

"A big one," agreed Grandma.

"Uh-huh," I agreed.

"Things are, shall we say, about to get messy." Grandma wiggled an eyebrow at Madge.

"Very," agreed Madge.

"Will you please get to the point?" I snapped, more frustrated than the time Faz wouldn't leave the house for our dinner date because he couldn't find the polish for his shoes.

"Okay, let me tell it," said Grandma.

"Fine," said Madge.

"We're old friends, go back a long way. Not that we see much of each other or let anyone know. Sometimes it's best to keep your friendships hidden."

"Why?"

"So your enemies don't use it against you," said Madge like it was obvious.

"I thought I was telling this?" said Grandma with a frown.

"Suit yourself."

"As I was saying. We're old friends, and we've noticed for a while that things haven't been quite right. There's a problem, and a big one, and…" Suddenly Grandma stopped dead, her eyes widened, and she gasped.

"What? What is it?"

"Where's the baby? Where's my great grandson?"

"Huh? He's with Delilah. He's safe, don't worry." I got a very bad feeling, and it didn't ease when Grandma spoke.

"What do you mean? You mean you haven't just hidden him around here?"

"No, are you crazy? I'm not going to hide a baby in the woods and chase around looking for kidnappers. That would be nuts."

"Oh, this is bad, very bad. We assumed when they took Faz and the others that you had Kane with you. They won't touch him, not yet, but now…"

"If you two don't start explaining this I swear I'll… Just tell me."

"Kane isn't what you think he is, Kate," said Grandma. "Nobody will touch him, they can't, but we assumed he was with you. Safe. It's all part of their plan, they'll be waiting."

"I swear I'll pick up this gun and shoot you both dead if you don't tell me what the hell you are talking about." I was on my feet and felt my eyes darken and the magic surge. Family or not, I would shake them until the words I wanted to hear fell from their wrinkly mouths.

"Kane is almost ready to change," said Grandma.

"Change? Into what?"

"Into a boy."

"He's already a boy."

"But not one who can walk and talk and use magic," said Grandma.

"Obviously. He's eight months old. Almost."

"Exactly. I think we better explain this properly," said Grandma. Madge nodded.

"About bloody time."

"There are forces afoot, evil forces that have been messing with our world ever since you discovered how to have a child. Once you were pregnant, things became almost out of control. We've been doing our best to deal with it, keep it quiet, but we can't do it alone. The goblins and their machine, Hidden acting strangely, everyone going funny in the head, making odd choices, like you coming here camping, all of it, it's all linked. All because of what you are, what Faz gave you. What could happen."

"And what could happen?" I didn't want to ask, but I had to. I had to know.

"It already has. You had a baby. A boy."

"So he's special, but he's perfect."

"He is. That's the problem."

"Look, this is stupid. He isn't a vampire, hasn't done anything peculiar at all. He's just a baby."

"No he's not," said Madge. "You know what I am, what I can do?" I nodded. "Kane will be able to do that and so much more. He will have magic, be powerful, and he—"

"This is my story," interrupted Grandma. The two women glared at each other as only old women who's friendship was based on bickering could do.

"Fine. Tell it then."

"Kane is special. You just don't know how special. He is what many have dreaded, what many have hoped for. He's everything."

"Everything?"

"He will change, and soon, and then you'll see. The magic grows in spurts until young adulthood, then it slows down to normal speed. But until then it will be tough. And it's almost time."

I didn't know what to think. It was like they'd lost the plot and were talking crazy. He was a baby, nothing more. Sure, the pregnancy had been odd, and brief, but that was because of the magic inside of me. We all expected him to be somewhat unique, to have inherited some of the Hidden magic Faz gifted me, but beyond that nothing. Just a Hidden child with power and access to the Empty like so many others of our kind.

"What's going to happen?" I asked with a whisper.

"He'll gain his power. In time, he will be incredible, a true force of nature. He'll have so much, become so much."

"A wizard?" I asked hopefully.

Grandma nodded. "Yes, and a shifter. And, a vampire."

I puked.

Information Overload

Grandma gave me a damp cloth and I wiped my face, then sat, feeling numb and unable to process what I was being told. Both women sat opposite me and said nothing, just glanced at each other and did a lot of eyebrow wiggling. With nothing left to lose, I focused myself as best I could and said, "Tell me. And don't mess about, just tell me what's really happening here."

"Okay, love. And I'm sorry, this isn't how I wanted things to work out. We thought you'd all be safe here, honest we did. It's why we came, to take care of you."

"But the huts, how did you set this up before you even knew we were coming? Our trip was spur-of-the-moment."

Grandma smiled her know-it-all witch smile and then things slotted into place.

"You suggested this place to Faz, didn't you?"

"Maybe," said Grandma with a wink.

"And the rest? What's going on? Who has them? What can I do to help Kane?"

"Firstly, Kane just needs you to be with him, to help him. We don't know what will happen, nobody does, and that's the point. But it will happen, and soon. You should go get him. Keep him close at all times."

"Grandma, you're frightening me."

"I know, and I'm sorry. We didn't think things would happen like this, but they have, so we need to adjust."

"I should go then, get Kane," I said, standing. I found myself cradling the gun like I already had him in my arms.

"But I haven't told you what this is really about yet," said Grandma gently, making me aware I was close to losing the plot.

"Ah, right." I sat, placed the gun down carefully, and tried to focus. "It's the vampires, right?" I said with a sigh, knowing it would be. It always was, always is, always will be.

"No, it's the witches. More specifically, a group of them. We don't know who, we've tried to find out, but we can't get information. Whoever it is, they're being secretive, working in a way that's sneaky."

"Witches are good at being sneaky," agreed Madge.

Grandma nodded. "We've had to be to get along in this world. Men always think they've got the upper hand, are running things, but they don't. We run things, women, and we know everything that goes on. There are rumors, that's it."

"This is why it's just you two?"

"Yes, love. I don't know who I can trust these days, so I've not said a word to anyone apart from Madge. We know they're here somewhere, we know they're up to something, we just aren't sure what."

"But you sent us here, knowing there would be danger?"

"No, I sent you here so we'd have help if we found them. I didn't expect them to take my grandson. I assumed that you all being here would act as a warning, maybe make them run, and we'd finally find out who it is, track them. Well, Madge could track them. Right, Madge?"

"Absolutely."

"But," Grandma scowled, "the buggers have gone too far. They've kidnapped Faz and the damn Head, and Persimmon. Even Mithnite. You don't mess with family. Not my family."

"This doesn't make sense. Why would witches do any of this? Why would they kidnap the others? What do they want?"

"It's obvious, isn't it? They want to rule."

"Rule what? The Council?"

"No, love, you don't understand. This isn't a power play to run the stupid Council. They want to be in control of everything. Come out of the shadows and rule the world."

"Haha, you mean like come out? Let Regulars know about us?"

"Maybe," said Grandma with a frown.

I stared from one woman to the other, trying to think this through, to understand what I was being told. Then something clicked and for a moment I was in two minds whether to say something or not. But I had to. How would I know what to do if I didn't have as much information as possible?

"You're making this up, aren't you? You're either lying to me or you haven't got a clue what's really happening. You don't know it's witches at all, you have no idea who it is but just think maybe it's witches as you haven't been able to find anything out. How do we even know there's anything going on?"

"Get her," whispered Madge, and for an instant her words didn't register. Get her? Get who?

Then, as Grandma snatched the machine gun and smacked me across the head with it and Madge leaped up and her body flickered into the form of a different person, and a man at that, I realized they meant me.

"Grandma?" I said in shock, then Madge's hands were on my throat, squeezing tight, and I couldn't breathe. Grandma slammed the butt of the gun into my temple.

I was out cold. I didn't expect to ever wake up.

I'm Alive!

Have you ever been smashed repeatedly about the head with the blunt end of a machine gun? No? Then I don't recommend that you go in search of such a thrill. It really hurts. Like, a lot. Being strangled has its down side too.

But I wasn't dead, which was good, as otherwise I'd have been stuck forever in limbo, unable to figure out what the hell had just happened.

Not that I knew what was going on when I came to my senses—what hadn't been knocked or strangled out of me.

My head felt like it had split open, and maybe it had, as there was certainly blood. My right eye was caked in it, and I struggled to open it as the blood had dried and stuck the lid like super glue. I would have raised my hand to feel for the cut and the bump, but the fact I was trussed up like a Christmas turkey made it impossible.

My temple throbbed and my throat felt raw, as if it had been crushed and hadn't repaired properly. Magic surged as I came to consciousness and I willed it to the damaged areas although it was already working away hard in the background. As I focused, so the pain eased, but it wasn't the temporary suffering that concerned me, it was that I'd been duped and feared for the life of my family.

These people weren't Grandma and Madge, that was for sure. They were something even scarier and more worrying, and if you knew these two women you'd know how hard it was to be scarier than either of them. These were doppelgängers, of the supernatural kind. A form of shifter, they are rarer than a vampire with no teeth, and for obvious reasons a lot more terrifying.

I tried to get my thoughts in order, to slot this piece of the puzzle into place, but I couldn't figure things out, didn't know how this fit together. Why had two doppels—yes, it's lazy but that's what they've always been called according to Faz—impersonated Grandma and Madge then told me all this weird stuff about witches being behind everything?

If my hand was free I would have slapped myself upside the head. Information, they did it to get information. They grabbed those dwarves and led me here so they could run this stupid bloody game on me and extract information. They wanted not only me, or maybe not me or any of us, they wanted my baby. My son. And I'd told them where he was, who had him.

Did they know who Delilah was? Of course they did. If they knew enough about me to impersonate Grandma and Madge then they knew who Delilah was and where she lived.

I felt sick again, and urged, but held it down and forced cooling, soothing, calming magic to sweep over me like a breeze. My heart slowed enough for me to think clearly, but I was so close to panicking and freaking out at the thought of them taking Kane that to this day I don't know how I remained in control under such stress. Maybe it was the vampire in me, the detached coldness finally being allowed to surface and scrub away, albeit temporarily, the love and compassion I hold in the highest regard. Had I brought myself a step closer to losing my emotions altogether? I don't know, and I don't care, for I would risk it all to protect my boy.

They'd fooled me, led me here to capture me and Kane. The only thing I could think was that they'd simply come to get us all and when I wasn't there they'd assumed Kane was with me. Maybe Faz had hidden him when he believed something was about to happen? Or, and this made me smile despite my predicament, maybe Faz had put Kane down for a moment and when our campsite was stormed Kane had hidden himself because he sensed danger.

Was what the doppels said true, or were they playing games with me? Was Kane about to become something different, to become a monster, or start showing signs of magical ability?

Why had they told me this? Why would they bother? I ran the conversation back in my mind and understood it was to get as much information from me as possible. It didn't make it true though, did it?

I had to escape and get Kane, and get him now.

For the first time since I became conscious, I realized I wasn't alone. Two men were sitting the other side of the fire, facing me, watching me, the pretense gone.

I hissed at them and my teeth snicked down hard, dripping the vampire's tear.

"I'm gonna rip your throats out and enjoy doing it."

The men smiled, opened their mouths, and morphed into perfect copies of me. Their eyes darkened, their canines shone, and they cackled.

Damn, but I'm a scary looking woman when I'm in vampire mode. I have to say, I was impressed.

Very, Very Weird

The two Kates laughed, faced each other, shifted back into male form, then conversed in a low whisper, ignoring me. Trying not to utterly freak out, I focused on my bindings, testing them against my strength and magic.

It was rope, but no rope I'd ever encountered. The strands were rough and to the eye appeared normal at first, but when I struggled they activated, shimmering with a white light. It writhed, responding to the pressure I exerted and pulling tighter at my hands, my body, and my neck where it held me rigid to what I could only assume was one of the large posts for the washing line.

Where were the good old dumb bad guys who never tied the rope properly, letting you make your hand small and slip out of your bindings? These guys were professionals, knew what they were doing, and they obviously knew magic to have bound me like this.

What did I know about doppels that I could use to my advantage? Actually, not a lot, only what Faz had told me, and he'd told me a little about a lot, but not a lot about much. This Hidden world is huge, and it is only by living in it, and for many years, that you become aware of just how vast it is. There is so much to know, so much to learn, and I'd hardly scratched the surface. Faz had recounted a tale about a job involving doppels, but he'd said nothing about them using magic. They were supposed to be like shifters, had inherent magic but weren't inclined or very adept at accessing the Empty. Somebody had obviously forgotten to tell these two.

Either way, it left me screwed.

Day turned to night. It grew cold out in the open even though the veil around the clearing would have kept it a few degrees warmer. The men disappeared now and then, going about whatever business they had, sometimes singly, sometimes together. They cooked, they ate and drank, they went inside the huts, and they refused to talk or give me anything to eat or drink. Then they left.

So rude!

The night brought with it a new set of terrors as my imagination ran wild, the emptiness above making me fear the worst. The men had been gone for hours. They must have been pretty confident to not want to keep watch over me. Had they gone to get Kane? They had, hadn't they. They'd be gone half the night if they drove, although I'd seen no sign of a vehicle. Maybe they had it stashed somewhere.

Again, I wondered how they'd managed to get us here, as we'd obviously been led to this place for our vacation. Had they somehow fooled Faz? Impersonated Grandma and told him about this place? It must have been something like that, which meant we could have been talking to them for who knew how long. Had I had discussions with my husband or Dancer or Persimmon, talked of business when really the doppels were getting valuable information? Had the others done exactly the same? How many other people of authority or importance had they been impersonating?

This was bad, very bad.

I began to sweat as I understood the consequences. They could return to Cardiff and pretend to be any of us. Were there only two doppels or were there many more? Were these two really twins? Was I seeing the true them or were they keeping their identities secret? So many questions. Right now, they could be impersonating Faz and Dancer. Hell, if one could look like the Head he could cause an insane amount of trouble for our city, for our kind.

Had they already been doing it?

Was my baby safe?

How could I escape?

Mind whirling, utterly exhausted, I must have dozed off eventually, as when I woke, my worst fears had become a reality.

Utter Terror

I was startled from my nightmares by the sound of my baby crying. I shook my head to clear what must have been part of my dream, and opened my eyes to discover that dawn had broken. The sky was clear and blue, not a cloud in sight, and it promised to be sweltering. I was already hot in my leathers, but as my eyes focused and the screaming refused to go away, all that was forgotten as my eyes locked on a small lump on the ground thirty feet away.

My baby.

I searched in a panic for the doppels but they weren't in sight. I shouted for them, I screamed, I begged, but they didn't come.

Kane grouched, then cried, wailing for his mummy. For me to come get him, save him and cuddle him, but I couldn't. I struggled until the rope threatened to choke me. I ignored the pain, but knew I'd be no good to him dead.

I shouted more, pleaded until I was hoarse, but nobody came, nobody answered my pleas, my begging. Kane wriggled about on the dusty ground, but he was too young to walk, too little to stand and take tentative steps. He was a baby, naked in the dirt, alone and terrified.

In a soothing voice, I called to him so he'd look my way, and slowly his wails and tears faded and he began to crawl to me. But if he came too close he'd touch the ropes, and they'd burn him, maybe kill him. I could cope, but only because of the constant background hum of my own dwindling magic.

Soon I'd be unable to protect myself, and I'd be overcome by my bindings, but Kane would be dead by then if he continued to crawl. He'd grab my feet, tug on a trouser leg, haul himself up and reach for my bonds. Then his soft body would be thrown back and he'd die in the dirt while I watched, unable to help my baby boy.

What sick, perverted torture was this?

"What do you want? What do you want to know? Please, you have to help him."

Kane crawled through the dust.

He smiled at me and I felt sick to my rotten core.

Nobody came.

No Respite

How could anyone do this to an innocent child? To my baby? Kane stopped at my shrill shriek, cocking his head to one side as if to decipher the meaning. He scratched at the dirt with his soft, fat fingers, put a fistful to his mouth and began eating it. Then he began to choke and I lost all control. My tears fell until my clothes were soaked, my throat rasped like a tube of sandpaper had been rammed deep down inside as I screamed, shrieked, and pleaded for somebody to come and help my baby.

His face turned red then purple as he made little gasping sounds, his chubby hands rubbing at his face, his small brain unable to understand what was happening or what to do.

I couldn't take my eyes off him but I was helpless, the worst feeling in the world. Kane toppled sideways and I was more afraid than I have ever been in my life as he lay there, silent.

Then he coughed and dirty liquid oozed from his mouth and he righted himself after a few attempts. He wiped at his mouth with a clenched fist, then smiled up at me with a twinkle in his eye like he'd just been playing a great game with mummy.

He crawled forward again, this time with renewed vigor and intent, arms and legs like squat pistons. In my mind he was speeding across the divide, faster than the vampire shimmer shuffle, but of course, he wasn't. His fat legs kicked and scooted as he made his way, all the while making cute sounds I knew meant he wanted a cuddle. He left a trail of wee behind him.

Still nobody came, and again I panicked and called for help as he got closer, knowing I was about to witness the death of my own flesh and blood, the most important, magical, stupendous thing in my life.

It was almost an out-of-body experience, as his death approached. I was above, looking down on him and on me tied to a damn post, unable to free myself. Yet for all that, for all that I felt impossibly pathetic and feeble, part of me wouldn't accept this as a reality. There was this hardness at my core that promised me everything would be okay, that somehow everything would work out all right. That he wouldn't really touch the rope that right now was half strangling me and burning my flesh over and over again, each time hurting a little more as my body failed to recover fully.

I refused to believe my child would die. It wouldn't compute, wouldn't fully register even though most of me understood that life was a bitch and bad stuff happened every minute of every day to millions of poor souls across the globe. Maybe it was because I'd been involved in so much, faced danger on numerous occasions, lived in a world where violence was never far away, and I'd come through it all relatively unscathed, a survivor.

Kane was going to die. I knew it but I couldn't believe it, a contradiction but what else can a mother do when faced with such horror? You have to believe everything will be okay if merely for your own sanity.

Something would happen at the last minute, something dramatic and epic and he'd be saved, me too. I struggled against my bonds, searching for a weak spot again, but the magic was too strong and I was too weak now. I was not going to get out.

Maybe Delilah would turn up in dragon form, blast the bad guys and grab Kane before it was too late. Or Faz would appear, negate the magic, and cut my bonds.

Something. Anything.

Kane stopped to play with his feet, in no way concerned with his situation now he'd had a while to get used to it. He put his toes in his mouth and murmured with contentment, but grew bored after a while and once again remembered that I was here and he still wanted a cuddle.

"No, Kane, Mummy's busy, go and play somewhere else," I said in as calm and soothing a voice as I could. He smiled at me and continued to crawl.

Frantic, with less than ten feet between us now, I searched the compound for any other signs of life but it was still as quiet as a ghost town. Was this real? Was I hallucinating? This couldn't possibly be happening. Nothing can prepare you for such torment, so I tried to believe this was just me dreaming, or some weird twisted magic designed to break me. Maybe I'd been drugged, given a potion to make me believe this.

I knew that was wishful thinking, though. Inside, I understood this was real, that this was Kane and I couldn't help him.

He was close now, five feet away, and he wasn't stopping.

What should I do? What should I say to him to make him stop? Something, anything.

I told him, "No," in a stern voice, but he was undeterred. I shouted at him, I spoke in a whisper, I even sang Baa Baa Black Sheep in the hopes he would sit on his dimpled bum to listen, but no, he sped up and squealed with delight at the movements of his body, pleased to finally get close enough for a hug.

Then he was at my feet, dragging at my boots. He clutched a fat handful of leather with a determined grip and hauled himself to his feet. I shook my leg, trying to kick him off, thinking a few bruises were preferable to death, but I was tied so tight that as soon as I tried to move the bindings cut through the leather deeper than ever and all I could do was move my ankle a little.

Consumed with horror, I watched my perfect, innocent little baby boy reach up to the sparkling ropes and grab hold.

The rope crackled with violent energy.

Kane shot backwards like a lightweight plastic doll and slid across the dirt on his back, screaming as his body blistered and tiny stones cut deep into his flesh.

Then he was still.

Life as I knew it was over. There was no point going on now, all hope was lost.

Darkest Despair

Kane's tiny, pale body was a mess of cuts and bruises, his hands were terribly burned, blackened and covered in fiery red blisters that popped and oozed. He looked impossibly small there, this part of me that consumed my entire existence, amazed me with how much love I had to give, thinking it wasn't possible to have such depth of emotion, to worship with such intense devotion.

Now he was dead.

Anger the likes of which I've never known surfaced and I let out an almighty, piercing cry of bottomless anguish that thundered through the clearing. With it came an outpouring of magic, fortifying my torment and sorrow with soul-tearing energy. The sound hit the veil and the entire thing vibrated and shone silver as sparks pulsed and the dawn turned black.

I was plunged into darkness, absolute, and I welcomed it, welcomed the respite so I didn't have to look at my son. Again I screamed, a cry for all the mothers in the world who had ever lost a child. A noise tinged with true Hidden magic, something primordial and base, the very essence of the universe.

The black veil bounced my sorrow back at me, magnifying it, until I didn't think I could stand it a moment longer. Then light poured in as the blackness melted away like hot water poured over ice, and the veil dissolved, leaving me open to the raw power of nature, the sounds of the birds.

A breeze ruffled the fine blond hair on Kane's head. His body was blue now.

Untold Strength

Through my tears I could make out indistinct figures at the edge of the clearing. For a moment I thought they were standing stones, or trees, but as the tears stopped I understood that they were people. A blast of hot wind dried my eyes and everything came into sharp focus, but I didn't want to look at anything, as I knew I'd stare at my baby, could never look away.

"The One. The One," came a chant, and I peered at the motionless figures, only for my despair to intensify as I stared at maybe thirty perfect copies of me.

"You fucking freaks. You're sick, the lot of you. Have you no pity, no shame? You killed my baby!"

Something went wonky in my body, or mind, I don't know which, and for a moment I was insane, I'm sure I was. I lost control of limbs; I lost control of everything. Blood magic surged from every cell and activated, bringing with it an impossible strength. Hidden magic joined in, fattening my ink and spitting from my skin as I twitched, my flesh burning and scarred as the rope tightened. I didn't care about that now, didn't care about anything, especially myself. I screamed in final, complete release and let the magic do as it would.

My skin split under the pressure as magic anguish burst from my chest, my abdomen, my arms, and legs. It spewed from my mouth in a fierce volatile torrent and my dark eyes bled tears of actual magic as my fangs dripped deadly poison and my hands stretched and the nails became claws of a sort. All the power I held within, more than I thought possible, all the rage and utter despair surged from my body until I was engulfed by it.

Maybe I'd find peace now, find oblivion.

Everything burned away, leaving me hollow inside and with only one purpose before I gave up this useless life once and for all.

I would destroy these monsters.

The bindings grew tight, my breathing was cut off, the ropes chewed down to the bone and I welcomed it. As my wounds flared with white fractal energy, the ropes, magical or not, failed, the power imbued in them not up to this level of violence. Then they were just plain ropes, burned away in a moment.

I was free, but at what cost?

I ran to Kane and picked up the bloodied, battered corpse of my little baby boy and hugged him to my chest as the magic faded as quickly as it had come.

"The One. The One," the doppels chanted, thirty of me circling the compound, closing in as they smiled and made me lose my mind.

"I love you," I whispered as I held Kane tight, too late to protect him.

His tiny body twitched, and I dropped him.

Oddness

I gasped as Kane's spasming body fell from my arms. Everything slowed down, and I watched as his death-twitch was repeated as he fell. But then he wasn't falling. As the body turned, he vibrated and was enveloped in a magical cocoon like a spider wrapping up its next meal in gossamer thread. He was imprisoned in untold strands of this silver energy, and he spun faster and faster, trapped in magic that suspended him parallel to the ground.

Hidden energy flowed from me to him, and from him to me, like a two-way umbilical cord, and I felt a glimmer of hope beneath the despair. The connection deepened and the magical aura intensified and then as suddenly as it began it stopped.

The cocoon split apart and a wave of supercharged energy swept over me and drew a gasp from the doppels, who were now a mere twenty feet away.

Kane hung sideways in the air, surrounded by a silver aura, spinning slowly. But it wasn't Kane, at least not my baby boy. This was a child of three, maybe four. Then five, then six, then eight, ten. Twelve.

Abruptly, the spinning stopped, and he curled up in a fetal position, knees tucked in tight against pale flesh. Brown hair hung long and curly, and then he dropped to the dust with an "Oomf."

"That hurt," came a muffled voice.

As I stood there in shock, a pair of bright blue eyes, impossibly large and full of love and a deep, intimidating hardness, looked into my soul.

"Hello, Mother," said my son.

Everything Goes Wonky

"Um, hello?" I ventured, unable to keep up with events, or get anywhere close to understanding what was happening.

The child on the floor shuddered and shook off magic like a wet dog, then he rose, naked and perfect, pale and flawless. He shone like an angel, melting my heart with joy, but I couldn't understand how this could be. It wasn't possible.

"The One," the doppels shouted once, but they didn't move, came no closer.

"Shall we leave, Mother?" asked Kane. He ignored the others, put out his hand.

In a daze, I took his slender fingers in mine and we gripped hard, like nothing could ever part us again.

His touch was electric, like a static charge, but it was also cold. I clutched tighter, ignored the tightening of my skin as it healed, then I staggered as pain stabbed at my mind. Guess I'd fried more than a few synapses with all this going on, and for the first time the magic was actually having to repair my mind. Reconfigure pathways so I didn't go hide in a dark corner somewhere and gibber nonsensically.

We had eyes only for each other, and I smiled at my son, sure of only one thing. That this was him somehow. He had my slightly large forehead, a snub nose of youth, and full lips. His hair was dark now, the chestnut locks giving way to lustrous black. He was slender, verging on skinny, and perfect in every way.

He smiled at me again but there was something going on behind those eyes. Deep thoughts, a decision made. Without warning he leapt at me, grabbed my face in his hands, and we toppled backwards. He pushed against my mouth with his forearm, forcing it open, and his touch sent a shockwave through my body, made my mouth twitch as the familiar tingling signaled that my teeth were about to descend and I'd be in vampire mode.

No, no, no. What was he doing?

I panicked. I squirmed and writhed and beat on his back with my fists, tried to roll him off me but he had impossible power and strength, easily held me fast. I would have to use true violence to defeat him but how could I hurt my baby boy?

"It's okay," he whispered into my ear. "This is how it's supposed to be." He shoved his arm harder against my mouth until I was gagging.

My teeth descended, pierced his skin.

Unwanted blood flowed and the vampire's tears circulated in my son's system.

Somehow, I knew he was right. That if we were to survive, if my son was to live, then he had to be burdened with this terrible thing. And, God help me, I did as he asked. I made my son into a monster.

Blood that was my blood spurted to the back of my throat as senses went into overdrive. I was awash with bloodlust, unable to stop myself, and power and anger surged along with a terrible sadness born of despair for what my child had done, what he had become.

He pulled away from me softly and held out his hand to help me up. I took it, and he hauled me to my feet. Kane stared at his arm where two angry red dots faded then were gone. My son's eyes turned blacker than my evil vampire heart, his teeth snicked down as he snarled, and he whirled on the doppels and said, "You hurt Mother."

We bonded in blood that terrible day. Mother and son, vampires both, tore through thirty copies of me, ripping out their throats and tearing their limbs off in a blood frenzy that took away our sanity. My body sang with the joy of it all, with the power it gave, the energy building until I thought I could stand it no more, so ecstatic was I to have such a release.

We drank our fill and became our true selves unencumbered by guilt or thought, just acting as we desired, as was right.

And then it was over, and we stood amongst the carnage of the dismembered, eviscerated, shredded corpses of thirty men and women. Blood soaked the pale dust, turning it dull red. Our bodies were scarlet, our eyes as dark and cold as the furthest reaches of the universe.

We became the void itself. We thrummed to the twang of creation.

Magic, it sure is full of surprises.

Beastly

We collapsed, exhausted yet impossibly energized at the same time. I wanted to sleep but I wanted to run screaming through the forests. I wanted to devour until I could kill no more, and I also wanted to throw up. I'd never felt such wildness, such overwhelming blood magic, and I'd never come so close to losing my sanity before. This was madness on an epic scale.

We sat in the center of a circle of mangled bodies, both of us panting. I watched the young boy beside me, covered in blood, head back, as he stared up at the sky.

"I'm sorry, Mother, but it had to be done. They were bad people, they had to be stopped. You wouldn't have won if you'd tried to kill them alone. This was the only way. I had to be vampire too, so we could be together. Shall we go and get Faz now?"

For a moment I failed to understand why he was talking about Faz. Get him? Then I remembered and I snapped from the bloodlust like I'd stepped into a cold shower. "You did this for me, to protect me?"

"For both of us, for Father too. For everyone. They told you I would change, didn't they? Told you this would happen?"

I nodded. "You heard?"

"I've been listening since before I was born. I know what you know, what Faz knows, and so much more besides. Sorry if I scared you." He looked like a young child again then, saying sorry as though he'd spilled a drink on the carpet or something, not grown into a juvenile, forced me to turn him, then torn copies of me to bits. It could worry you, a psychoanalyst would certainly have a field day with all this.

"My poor son. You're changed forever now, you know? You're vampire and you'll have to feed."

"But only from the list, right?"

"Only from the list," I agreed. "How?" I whispered, finding it hard to breathe let alone talk.

"Because of the magic Faz gave you, of course."

"You should call him Father, or maybe Dad. He won't like being called Faz." Seemed however shocked and confused I was, I was still in mum-mode.

"Haha, maybe Father. But Faz sounds cooler." Kane chuckled and I laughed a little despite the enormity of all this.

"Maybe."

"As to how, your magic made me something unique, Mother. These doppels, they did this on purpose. Thought I was the One, whatever that means. They brought me here and tormented you, knowing that when I died I would be reborn, that the touch of magic that strong would start the metamorphosis."

"How? How did they know this?"

"Because they have a prophecy, believed it too. So stupid."

"Lots of people have wondered what you would be like, if you'd be touched by magic. And a few nutcases have come in search of you, claiming you're their leader, their salvation." There had been a veritable queue of nutters seeking us out, wanting to see Kane, speaking of their prophecies and their peculiar beliefs. Others wanted nothing to do with me or Faz because of Kane, others hated me because of what I'd gone through to become pregnant

"I know. I heard."

"From before you were born? How is that possible?"

Kane shrugged his skinny shoulders. "Life's weird."

"You got that right. These doppels, they knew you'd change when you got hurt badly or killed? So they set this up? This was their plan all along?"

"That's what I could gather from what they said after they took me. After they tricked Delilah."

Delilah! I'd forgotten about her. "Is she okay? Did they kill her?"

"No, nothing like that. One pretended to be you. Delilah was confused, but she handed me over. The doppel said she couldn't bear to leave me with her, and that Faz was already safe, at home. I missed a lot of it, didn't hear as I was in the other room, but they got me and brought me back so I'd lead them."

"Can you, you know?"

"Do what they do? Mother, I can do things you haven't even imagined."

My son stood and he became Faz, then me, then Grandma, then the beautiful Persimmon. Then a panther, then a dog, and on and on in a dizzying blur of shifts that left me gasping and sad to the core of my corrupt soul.

"Why are you crying?" asked Kane as he stopped the show.

"My poor son. You poor thing."

"Mother, don't you get it? This is nothing to be sad about. This is wondrous. This is something to celebrate."

"Your first act as a boy has been to kill and become a vampire. I think that's something to be sad about."

"It was them or us. It hurts to take lives, I feel that, know how wrong it is, but they were bad people, would have used me in terrible ways. Now they are dead."

He said it so matter-of-fact; I understood then that it would take a long time before I understood this child, this boy. But then, we had all the time in the world, didn't we?

Numb, going on instinct alone, I searched the area and found where they'd left the cars. I drove a minibus back, and we piled up the bodies inside then spent a while spreading fresh dirt over the blood until the area was clean. Then we washed in a nearby stream, took clothes from the vehicles, and dressed.

I wasn't hungry or thirsty, I'd had my fill from blood, the same as Kane.

We headed off into the wilderness to find the others. I realized I'd never get to see my son take his first baby steps, teach him how to eat proper food, laugh as he pronounced words wrong or a million other things every parent gets to live through.

I'd missed out on so much, and I'd never get that time back.

A Wander

Kane had no more idea than me where the others could be, so we headed back to our camp site. It was weird returning. The tents were still up, Dancer's car was there, the camp fire too. The first thing I did was take off a dead woman's clothes and change in the tent. Kane took some of Faz's, going for a pair of jeans and black t-shirt I'd persuaded Faz to bring as who the hell goes camping in a suit? He'd brought them, but wore his suit anyway. The muppet.

Changed, feeling more myself again in jeans and a white t-shirt, I was overcome with a deep lethargy. Kane seemed exhausted too, dark bags under his eyes. Eyes, I reminded myself, that several hours ago were those of a baby, now of a boy approaching teenage years in appearance.

It was too much for the both of us, and before we had a chance to consider how wise it was to rest, we flopped onto the sleeping bags in the boiling hot tent and promptly fell fast asleep. I did not have nice dreams.

Action

Sweat stinging my eyes startled me from my slumber with a start. I sat bolt upright and tried to get my mind to work. Surely that had all been a bad dream? Nope. Judging by the way my system thrummed with wild energy, and the boy asleep beside me snoring exactly like Faz did, it had been nothing of the sort.

My son had done what I'd seen, was real, was here, and looked so much like his father I found myself weeping with joy and with sorrow so deep the ache in my heart became unbearable.

Quietly, I left the tent.

What was I supposed to do now? Was there anything I could do? Would Kane suddenly turn into a grown man, or an old one? He'd said this was it, hadn't he, but how did he know? Because he was special, that was why. He was unique in the whole Hidden world, something unheard of, but clearly dreamed of by the doppels, or this group of them anyway. Why was he of such interest to them in particular? Because of his ability to shift, I assumed. These doppels were limited to human form, but Kane was so much more. They wanted a mighty leader, someone to give them power. Nobody trusted doppels, and from what I'd been told, most were off the charts batty, unable to cope with the changes they could make.

Hardly surprising, and you couldn't blame them for that. How it must mess with your head and your body image when you could look in the mirror and see a stranger staring back at you. No wonder most were quite mad, dangerous too. It's a hard thing to accept, as you always want to think the best of people, but there was something wonky in doppels' genes. Along with the ability, there was a flaw in the system that meant most became unstable during childhood, then dangerous. They stuck to their own limited kind as they grew up because nobody else came close to understanding them.

My knowledge was very limited though. I had just been told that they had a hard time in the world and that they were rare beings, which was a good thing.

My son could do what they did, my son could shift into animal form, my son had inherent Hidden magic he would undoubtedly learn to harness like me and his father, and, heaven help me, he was a vampire.

I'd made him a vampire.

No, that wasn't right. He'd made me make him a vampire. To save me, and himself. Maybe save us all.

His childhood was gone, I could never get it back. Soon he would be a man, the years flashing by in the blink of an eye, so after a lot of moping, plenty of regrets, and copious tears, I made a promise to myself as I sat on a dodgy folding chair under the beating sun. I would cherish every moment I had with Kane. I may have missed out on a lot, but there were many, many years ahead for us all to enjoy. I would be there for him when he needed me, would help him through this—if he needed my help—and ensure that above all else he knew he was loved.

What else could I do?

Doubts, even regrets, clouded my mind as I sat alone, body still sore and burning. Had we done a terrible thing having a child? Bringing Kane into a world unprepared for him, and him for it? Should we have ensured I never had a child, knowing there was a chance he'd be different to other human Hidden?

No, because then he wouldn't be here, and even though I didn't know this person, I wanted to. I wanted to be his mother and knew I had brought something wondrous into being.

I also understood that the world would never be the same again. Our lives would be different from now on. Kane would become powerful and dangerous, already was, and that would piss off a lot of Hidden. Look what had happened already. Look what humans had done to him.

What would be next?

I turned at the sound of the tent zip being opened, and smiled. Kane staggered out, hair disheveled, looking cute and sleepy.

"Hello, Mother."

"Hello, my son."

I knew one thing then. I'd protect him with my life, and I loved him. Okay, two things.

Getting to Know You

It was, to say the least, a peculiar time. We sat for a while and chatted, and now the situation was calmer we were both more relaxed in each other's company. We laughed a little, we spoke of what had happened, and Kane explained what he was, at least as far as he understood it.

From what he'd overheard, this had happened in the past to several children born of humans with true Hidden magic, but never to a vampire. Humans lucky enough to have been gifted true Hidden magic had born a child powerful at birth. That magic manifested in different ways. But they all had one thing in common. They had the ability to morph from baby into juvenile after six months or so of life, then aged normally.

The process was kick-started by extreme danger or their own apparent death. How anyone knew this would happen was a mystery and may have been the result of people trying to destroy such children. Kane had no answers, only knew what he'd heard from the doppels.

Nobody had told me any of this, but I guess that didn't mean nobody knew it was a possibility. If anyone would know it would be Dancer or Oskari, probably Grandma too. Had they all been keeping this information from me? Trying to keep it a secret and let Kane grow as other children do? Maybe.

But if Oskari knew, then he really would have a vested interest in keeping Kane and me close. Which, now I discussed it with Kane, I realized he'd done. Had this been his plan all along? Keep me happy, the first vampire to have a child for a very long time, as not only was that unique in and of itself, but so Kane could become what he had? It was more than Oskari could have asked for. Yet even he wouldn't have guessed that Kane would become vampire, nobody could have known that. I became convinced that all the major players knew he would be special, just not quite how special.

So here I was, getting to know my magical, vampire son, who'd been alive for mere months but had already killed, and probably had more life experience than most Regular adults.

I kept glancing at him when he stared off into the distance. He looked so serious when he was thinking, and I wondered what was going on in his head. However much he'd learned as he absorbed information like osmosis throughout his gestation and brief infancy, he was, when you got right down to it, still an innocent.

I'd do my best to keep him that way.

"Come on, let's go find your father," I said, standing and holding out my hand to him.

He took it and rose. "I know just how to do it, too. Don't be scared, Mother, this is natural for me." With that, Kane removed his clothes, dropped to all fours, and shifted into a jolly looking bloodhound. For the next few minutes I watched with a mother's worried eyes as my son sniffed the camp and headed back and forth down the various trails, returning then running off in different directions as he followed up on scents no human could discern.

One track he took saw him gone for fifteen minutes and I hardly breathed the whole time, a million worries crowding my mind. I cursed the bloodlust; if we'd kept a doppel alive maybe we'd have got information, saved ourselves all this stress. Finally, he returned, morphed back into the beautiful boy he was, and dressed.

"Come, Mother, I have found their trail."

So we packed up some supplies, made sure to take the machine gun and revolvers, and anything else deadly I could find—although this mother and son were probably the most deadly weapons of all—then headed off on our rescue mission.

What a Difference a Day Makes

They'd been missing for over forty eight hours now, although it felt like several lifetimes. From trolls to dwarves to doppels, rescue by dragon and my son growing up, it was enough to send you batty if you dwelt on it. But, strangely, or maybe I'd just had years of practice with weirdness, I was adjusting rapidly to this new set of circumstances.

Kane was, as I knew he would be, a great boy. He was funny, he smiled a lot, and he also asked several billion questions. Like, constantly. People had told me that children of two or three drove their parents bonkers with their incessant whys, and I was beginning to understand what they meant. Kane wanted to know about anything and everything. How did plants grow? What was the sun? How did trees work? Where did clothes come from? All of it.

Anything he hadn't heard explained either inside or outside the womb, he asked about. And trust me, that's a lot of stuff. What he would have learned gradually over the years, he wanted to understand immediately, and I didn't have answers for many of his questions.

Some things we just accept, don't even understand ourselves, so how do you go about explaining it to an inquisitive child? You don't, you struggle and try to think about it, only to realize you have no clue how bees make honey although you're sure you heard something about them taking the nectar back to the hive and being sick and that's what honey actually is, although that can't be right, can it? So gross.

After a while, I began to suspect he was messing with me, winding me up on purpose. Hadn't he said he knew everything me and Faz did? That he'd awoken to consciousness in the womb with our combined knowledge and experience already ingrained? I looked at him suspiciously, and he just smiled, his eyes twinkling. We laughed. He was a good boy, a joker like his father.

Every half hour or so, Kane would morph back into canine form and be gone for five minutes then return and continue to lead the way. We traveled higher into the mountains, where the forests gave way to rough, rocky terrain, like a repeat of the day before with the troll. Except this time I went much further from the routes the hikers were likely to take.

It took its toll, our legs unaccustomed to such exercise, especially Kane's, who hadn't even walked before today. How that was even possible neither of us knew, but walk and climb he did, so it just had to be accepted.

High on a windswept peak, with magnificent views of the Welsh countryside all around us, Kane disappeared once more. He returned excited, wagging his tail and panting, his ears flapping comically. What a life, watching your son behave in such a way. I think if I'd allowed myself to ponder it too deeply I'd have curled up in a ball and cried. But I had to remain strong, I had to focus, and I had to find Faz.

I had to find a way to process all this too, but that would have to wait until I knew we were safe, which I prayed we would be one day.

The wind tussled my hair and cooled my exposed skin as I thought of the chaos that awaited us back home. Oskari would have a field day with this, a Hidden vampire child able to do so much more than I possibly could. Or would he do all he could to destroy Kane, because of the danger he presented to Oskari's own dominance? Or maybe he'd just try to coerce Kane into working for him, want to train him in the ways of the cold, ruthless vampire? There were other possible reactions from the Hidden world, but not a single one of them would end well as far as I could tell.

I'd keep it secret, not tell another soul that Kane was vampire. No, that wouldn't work. Vampires of any age could sniff out their own kind a mile off. The connection was too strong between us all for Kane to hide his nature. So they'd just have to deal with it, suck it up and keep their bloody cold hands to themselves. Or else.

"I think I've found them, at least where they've been taken," said Kane, already back in human form and dressing.

"Great. Let's go."

Female Intuition

Kane led us through a series of sharp outcrops where a surprisingly good path was hidden between the rocks. It was smooth, wide enough for two, and had clearly been carved into the rock by experts. Namely, dwarves.

The air took on a strange glow, signifying the transition between one world and the next. This was both the Regular world and Hidden. Not a true leap into the unknown, but a finely balanced merging of the two realities, us able to move seamlessly between worlds because of our own Hidden nature. No Regular could follow this path, they'd lose their way and return, stopped in their tracks somehow. This was for those of our kind, a link for the dwarves between the realms.

I guess this was where the dwarves I'd encountered the previous day were headed. Where they felt safe, where the weight of mountains above their heads comforted them. Can't say I'm a fan really, as every time I'm in a cave something freaky happens, and as the path widened I knew for a fact that was exactly where this was heading.

"It's in here, I can smell it," said Kane as he sniffed the air, the effects of shifting still enhancing his senses.

"Wait," I shouted, my heart skipping a beat as he ran around the corner.

I got a very bad feeling, and one thing in this life that's as guaranteed as taxes is that bad shit happens when you least want it to.

Alone Again

I ran after Kane into what I expected to be an approach to another damn cave, but as I turned the corner the rock closed in overhead, my body tingled, and I found myself in a mine shaft. It was dark, it was warm, it was quiet. It was bloody annoying.

"Kane, where are you?" I called in a panic, but he didn't answer. The only sound was the dripping of water.

I took several steps forward, my enhanced vision bringing the shaft to life as everything took on a green glow and the image cleared. Yep, definitely in true dwarf territory now. The shaft was just over seven feet high and fifteen wide, expertly carved from the rock with regular supports. I was standing on wooden crossties that held a steel track, and my first thought was that this wasn't built to bring things up and out into the world, it was to take them down. Dwarves did all their work deep in the bowels of the earth, and that included extracting ore, although what they were usually after was their one true love. Gold.

I dared not move for fear of losing Kane to some stupid twisted mix between worlds, and panic set in as I stood there scanning the shaft that disappeared into pitch black several feet ahead. I strained my ears to the max, my motherly instinct in overdrive, certain he was here and hadn't stepped across an impossible-to-discern divide into yet another realm.

"Mother," I heard echoing up the shaft toward me, and I broke from my trance like a bullet from a gun. Every muscle in my body fired as I sped down the tunnel, shaft, whatever the damn dwarves called it, and hurtled into the darkness.

The moment I moved, body a blur of pure strength, lights sprang to life along the walls at dwarf head height. Hundreds of medieval torches lighting the way ahead. I sped past, the flames flickering in my wake, then I hit something, grabbed hold, and stared into the abyss.

I was at the top of a very steep, very awesome descent, and as I clutched the small tram, the lights highlighted the tracks like a roller coaster straight to hell.

"Uh, here goes," I whispered. Grabbing the rail, I released the brake, pushed hard, then jumped in.

I tried not to enjoy myself, honest I did. My son was gone, my family who knew where, but riding a dwarven tram down expertly laid tracks, plunging into darkness and your way lit moments before you arrive so its a constant surprise, well, it is kinda fun.

The g-force was so strong it felt like the hairs were being dragged from my head, yet I picked up speed as the angle grew sharper until I expected to tumble out the front. The fun bit was short-lived, definitely over. I glanced behind to see that the lights extinguished as soon as I passed, so maybe this was where Kane had gone. Had someone taken him or had he fallen into a tram and was just having his first ride?

Knowing the way of these things, someone had taken him for sure, and as freaked as I was, I willed the tram to speed up, to catch up with him. Down, down I sped, faster and faster until I couldn't have been far from terminal velocity, then the way became smooth as the track eased into a gentle curve.

This was either one hell of a large shaft or I was in a massive open cavern now, but knowing how the dwarven realms worked, at least according to Faz and Mithnite, I knew that anything could, and probably would, happen.

I wasn't wrong.

Welcome to Hell

All I could see were the lights moments before I passed, with glimpses through the track to darkness. I was on a narrow bridge, trundling along. I could have been inches from the ground or miles, I had no way of knowing. The sound of the wheels echoing made me believe I was very high up, and with a lot of space above and below, but it was just a guess.

Who had taken Kane now? More doppels, of course. But what were they doing down here, and how had they won the dwarves over? They wouldn't have, so that meant either the dwarves weren't in this area, or they were and the doppels had... That's where I faltered. I could think of no way in which the doppels could have defeated the dwarves and been left to do as they pleased.

What then? Dwarves had Faz and the others? But that made no sense either as the doppels who had taken me, who'd forced Kane to become a young boy, acted as though they were still very much in control.

Ugh, what a mess. I needed answers, so I guessed I'd keep on keeping on and soon enough I'd get what I was looking for. And anyone in my way was sure as sugar gonna get what they had coming.

Newly determined, refusing to be a victim, and somehow keeping my rising sense of panic and foreboding under enough control to allow me to function, I faced the darkness.

And promptly smacked into a very literal wall.

A split second before the end of the line hit in a very physical way, the wall ahead was lit up by a series of torches set in a circle. It was very pretty, but there was no time to appreciate its beauty. The tram careened into a solid barrier of steel and wood with its buffers, and I flew straight at the wall.

Magic panic-surged, I braced, knowing I was gonna break a lot of bones, and winced as I closed my eyes, waiting for the pain.

After several moments when nothing happened, I risked opening my eyes, only to find I was hurtling along a horizontal shaft. Strange forces eddied around me, as if moving not because of the momentum I'd accrued but because of something else.

I flailed as up became down, down became up, and I lost all sense of direction, only to discover moments later that I was dropping down a vertical shaft. The ground came up at me fast, and it looked hard. Again I braced in anticipation of broken bones, and readied my throat for expert screaming.

I slowed, then came to a gentle halt as twitching toes touched the ground. A pool of ambient light that came from nowhere yet was everywhere chased shadows away. I was in the middle of a complex series of patterns carved directly into the polished rock, circles and wandering lines that all converged where I stood.

"I'm definitely not in Kansas any more," I told myself. Although I was no Dorothy, there were sure to be several wicked witches coming to get me.

I waited, expecting something, but I didn't know what, and when nothing nasty attacked, nobody threw anything hard and heavy at me, and nothing got sliced off, I went to try to figure out what to do next.

The cavern was vast, or more a series of caverns I guess. Massive vaulted things supported by immense carved pillars the size of ancient oaks and just as gnarled looking. This was the home of the dwarves, where they felt most comfortable, where logic-defying rooms contained untold treasures. Where each dwarf had their own private hoard room, where they met and planned, lived, loved, and eventually died, many of them never once stepping foot above ground or even considering it.

I knew little of these realms, insofar as how any of it was structured, and I'm not sure anyone really does. What I did know was that it was all somehow connected, that many millions of these creatures lived in separate zones, almost mimicking the world above, so they could be in different continents so to speak, but that there were ways from one to the next. It was one world, a large conglomeration of caves and caverns, passageways and strange shafts that meant dwarves were never truly isolated.

Something like that anyway, although there were definite regional differences between the dwarves. They had regular fights, sometimes continent-wide wars, to settle grudges that never got settled and went so far back in the annals of time that nobody even knew what they were fighting about any more, just that they hated a certain bloodline and that was good enough for them. Yeah, sounds familiar doesn't it? In many ways they're very human, in others not so much.

Lost to my thoughts and indecision, I looked down as something tugged at my leather jacket. A rosy face with chubby cheeks and one hell of a beard and head of hair piled up in a thick ponytail like coiled rope smiled up at me.

"All right?" he asked.

"Um, been better. You?"

"Yeah, great. Fancy a drink?"

Confused, somewhat bemused, and definitely with nothing to lose, I said, "Sure, sounds, um, nice," and then was taken by a very calloused and strong hand and led away.

If nothing else, it was nice to have company.

A Reunion

I was dragged over to a door, with more studs than were strictly necessary, that I was sure wasn't there a moment ago, but that could have just been me not focusing, as I was rather out of sorts. The grinning dwarf twisted on a large metal ring and pushed the door open.

Inside was Kane, sitting on a wooden stool at a small table with several other dwarves. They all turned and smiled as we entered.

The first dwarf ushered me inside and slammed the door shut.

"Kane, are you okay?" I asked as I rushed over and hugged him. I also had a terrible urge to lick my finger and wipe the smudges off his face, but managed to control myself.

"Sure, Mother. Nice here, isn't it?" he said, smiling at me and nodding at the dwarves.

"It is now." I hugged him again, just because I am his mum and am allowed to, then turned and scowled.

"What's this all about? Where are my friends and my husband?"

"It's okay, don't get cross," said Kane, utterly calm and relaxed when I was ready to rip off heads or do something really nasty.

"Don't get cross! They kidnapped you, they must be working with the doppels. Look what they made you do. What they made me do. Look what they've done!" I screeched, getting seriously worked up.

"Oi, calm it, old lady," said one of the dwarves at the table as he, or maybe she, grabbed the double-headed axe resting against his leg and waved it in front of me menacingly.

"Oh, yes, okay, I'll just be all calm and friendly shall I after you lot stole my son and my family and sent me flying at a wall and down a shaft and have been working with those devils that did despicable things to me and made my son turn into a—"

"Mother!" Kane's sharp tone made me stop mid-sentence. I turned to him, aware I was losing the plot and getting a little what Faz calls "shouty and mental sounding." I call it passionate.

"Sorry. Okay, let's start again. What the fuck is happening here?" I may have let the magic ripple, and I may have begun to send off fierce sparks of menace, and everyone may have jumped up and stepped away and begun to mutter and say what a bad idea this was and they should never have interfered, and other confusing things. Then I may have just crumpled in on myself and slumped to the floor and begun to cry, but to be fair it had been a trying few days.

Actually it's been a trying lifetime, but it could have been worse.

"Who are you calling old lady?" I growled, but my heart wasn't really in it, so I went back to crying.

Things got a little awkward for a while. I sat there, uncomfortable with the gun still strapped across my back, dwarves milled about in the cramped, sparse room, and Kane just drank what smelled like cocoa. I wondered if there were marshmallows.

"Thought you said she was all fierce and scary?" a dwarf asked Kane.

"She is. She's just having a moment."

"I am not having a moment!" I shrieked, "I'm having a meltdown in the corner as this is too much to take. I don't know what's happening."

"Should we, er, give 'er a mo to get it together?" asked another dwarf, shifting from foot to foot and scratching at the ground with his axe.

"No, I'm fine. Sorry." I got up and straightened my clothes, dragged my fingers through the birds nest on top of my head, wiped my eyes, and did my best to smile.

"So, who's going to tell me what's happening?"

Everyone began speaking at once, and although dwarves aren't usually big on sentences over five words, this was obviously worth talking about as I was bombarded with a torrent of sound that made me want to chop my ears off and throw them down a very deep, very quiet shaft somewhere.

"One at a time, please."

The dwarves huddled up, and after several minutes of heated discussion and several playful knocks on the head with each other's axes, they broke with a grunt. One who looked slightly more grizzled than the rest, which trust me, was no easy thing, stepped forward solemnly and said, "I shall regale you with our story of woe, M'lady," and even did a little bow.

"Wow, um, okay. Don't get out much, do you?" I asked.

"Not in the last few centuries, no. Been busy with —"

I put up a hand. "Don't tell me, mining for gold?"

The dwarf frowned, then his eyes sparkled and he said, "How did you know? Are you a seer?"

"Nope, I just took a wild guess. Now, what's this all about?"

It took a while, dwarves like their tales long and they like to embellish them with dragons coming out of nowhere, ogres suddenly appearing for no good reason, and every few sentences they have to get in a few words about gold. Oh, and axes, and there's a lot of talk about how great beards are too.

We got there in the end, and it wasn't anything that cheered me up.

The Caretakers

"So you're caretakers?" I asked after what felt like several extended, bordering on infinite, lifetimes.

"Yeah. And it's boring," said the oldest dwarf, who, along with the others, refused to give out his name because they'd made a vow.

"And the dwarves that the doppels killed were just young kids? They'd been sent to help you out because they'd been naughty?"

"Already told you, didn't I? Stupid buggers ran off, now look what's happened."

"Mother, we should go. It's time to get Father and the others," said Kane who was now on his fourth hot chocolate and could have probably gone for another one. No, there weren't any marshmallows.

I stood and slid my coat on, strapped the gun and backpack on, and readied to leave.

"Wait," said a hairy, height-challenged warrior.

"Why?"

"We haven't told you what's happened yet."

I sighed. "I assumed you didn't know, as you've just spent an hour telling us you've been made to look after this abandoned area so another group of dwarves can't have it. That you've been here for decades as punishment for an unspecified thing you did, and that all you know is that there are bad people about the area, according to what you've heard from your listening posts, and that's about it."

There were a lot of sideways glances, and a lot of shuffling of feet, tugging of beards, and scraping of battle axes. "Well, am I wrong?"

"Er, well, now you put it like that, guess that is it."

"Come on, Kane, let's go." I turned to leave but Kane grabbed my hand and said, "Wait. They must know where they are." He turned to the dwarves and asked, "Do you? Do you know where everyone's been taken?"

"Course we do. Why didn't you just ask?" said their spokesman.

"Oh, for fu—" I stopped myself swearing for Kane's sake.

"It's okay, Mother, I've heard you swear lots of times."

"That was before I knew you were listening," I snapped. "Sorry, I'm a bit stressed."

"Moody, isn't she?" said a dwarf I was beginning to dislike even more than the others.

"I am not moody. I am stressed. Now, pretty please, with sugar on top. Where is my husband?"

"He's in that place called Cardiff. We got a shaft around here somewhere that will take you right there. It'll only take a couple of days to get to it, wanna see?"

"Cardiff," I spluttered. "They took them to Cardiff? How do you know?"

"The other night, when that dragon came and then drove off with the baby, some followed her, but the rest, the proper ones in charge, they took everyone to another place in Cardiff. Looked nasty it did, real beat up they were."

"But alive?"

"Oh yeah," chuckled the dwarf. "Definitely alive. You should've heard the language from the girl with the big ti… er, the large mammary glands us dwarves have no interest in whatsoever. And the one with the weird pointy shoes, he was hurling all kinds of abuse even though he was a right mess. Then they all, well, they was quiet after… er, after—"

"After what?" I asked, just about at the end of my tether.

"After they said they had his son and wife. Shut right up so he did."

I took in what they were saying, but something didn't quite ring true about this. How could these dwarves, supposedly from underground, see and hear so much? And why the hell didn't they help? So I asked them exactly that.

More scraping of axes along the ground, more cautious glances, more mumbles. Then another huddle, more grumbles and mumbles while Kane and I looked on, utterly perplexed and confounded by these strange characters.

"Break," they grunted, and they did. Break, that is.

"Right, now, this is a bit awkward wot with you being humans and all. Goes against tradition and you gotta promise not to tell. We're in enough bother as it is. If word got out that we showed—"

"Just get on with it," I sighed, wishing I'd never gone camping, and promising myself this was the last time. Unless the weather was extra nice, but definitely not Snowdonia. Somewhere else, somewhere abroad.

"Follow us," the dwarves chorused, as they marched away.

Kane and I exchanged a look, shrugged, and followed. What else could we do?

Ooh

"You have got to be kidding me," I gasped, so stunned I had to stoop and lift my jaw off the ground.

"This is unusual, right?" asked Kane.

"Yeah, very."

The dwarves skittered about, peering around pillars and into dark spaces, then huddled again, broke, and approached. Their leader said, "You promised not to tell. No human has ever been allowed to see, to know of this. If you tell, we'll be in terrible trouble."

"The worst," agreed the one I was now sure was female.

"Punishment beyond compare awaits. They'll take all our gold." They all shuddered—a fate worse than death.

"We won't tell, we promise. This is what I think it is, right?" I asked, knowing the answer but wanting confirmation.

"If what you're thinking it is, is the Listening and Looking Room, then yes. If what you're thinking is, er, something else, like, er, a room that isn't for looking and listening, then no." The leader fiddled with his beard. They definitely aren't big on imagination.

"Can we see? And listen?" asked Kane.

Again with the huddle, which was becoming annoying and time-consuming. Time we didn't have.

"Yes," came the reply, after the requisite hitting of heads, mumbling, and bickering.

The room was vast, meaning, you couldn't see the edges. At the same time it was cramped, rammed with what I can best describe as long curved horns that ended with large open ends. These were no normal horns though, they stretched up and up until lost to what looked like clouds in this seemingly infinite room.

Each horn was different. Fat, narrow, ridged, or smooth as silk. Others were lumpy, many were intricately carved. There were thousands of them, and I think maybe tens of thousands. Maybe millions. Each stopped at dwarf head height, but as I approached one it rose and the wide open end turned upward and latched to my ear. It wasn't unpleasant, more like putting a shell to your ear. But this was no sound of the sea I was hearing, it was a conversation. A very private, very smutty conversation. I pulled away and the horn bent down then was still.

"If you want to see, you have to turn your head and it will pop over an eye. Any eye, you get to choose."

"Um, no thanks, I'm good." I pulled Kane close before he saw or heard something a boy of his age shouldn't. Yes, I'm aware of the vampire massacre we performed, but I'm his mother and he was, and shall forever remain, my baby boy. Plus I said so.

"This is for the north-western quadrant. Covers Europe, a bit of what you lot call America, couple of other places. You can just do it random, or you can choose cities, streets, houses, any of that stuff. You gotta promise not to tell."

The dwarves were sweating now, and I could tell they were regretting their decision. Axes kept moving in twitchy hands, and I wasn't a hundred percent confident they wouldn't chop off our heads soon.

"I promise. I'll never tell another soul."

"Me either," said Kane, hand on heart.

It seemed to appease them for now, but for how long I wasn't sure. Best to get this over with quickly.

"Can you show me them? Where they are?"

"Um, afraid not. We kind of lost 'em, not that we were keeping a close eye anyway. You'd be amazed what goes on, and it's easy to get distracted what with all the, er…" He began to turn red, what little of his face I could see.

"He's a right perv," said the female crossly.

"Okay, where did you last see them?"

"They was in a black van going into the city, that's all we know. But that helps, right?"

"It does, it really does. Thank you." I finally felt like I was getting somewhere, even if that somewhere was right back home where I could have just gone days ago. It was time to leave.

"Say, don't suppose you've got a shaft that can take us back to our campsite have you?"

More huddles, more breaks, then a simple nod. With that, the ground disappeared from beneath us. I grabbed for Kane, clutched his hand tight, and we fell.

Bloody dwarves.

Like a Hedgehog

I pushed aside the leaves, feeling like I was coming out of hibernation, and dragged myself out of the narrow tunnel entrance where the roots of an oak had tangled through the rock. Once freed and on my knees, I reached in and hauled Kane through. I was sure he'd grown bigger.

"You need to improve your tracking skills," I said crossly, then realized that was a bit harsh as it was his first time. "Um, I mean good job on the tracking. Shame you followed dwarf scent instead of Faz's."

"Sorry, I was following a Hidden scent, I knew that, but I suppose I do need to practice." Kane smiled and I did the same, then checked out where we'd emerged.

I recognized where we were immediately, so we headed back to camp just a few minutes away. Wasting no time, and with at least some idea where to go, I went into the tent and changed, again, got clothes for Kane.

He emerged wearing more of Faz's casual gear, a little large, but a decent enough fit.

"You look just like your father," I said, still unable to accept that this fine young man before me was my baby boy.

"Father would want to wear a tie though, right?" Kane smiled, and tugged at the collar of the black polo shirt.

"Haha, he would. All he wanted to bring were suits. Come on, let's pack up and get back to the city. I don't know what we'll find there, but there's nothing for us here now."

Twenty minutes later the tents were put back in their bags—okay, they were sticking out. How come tents never fit back in the bags they came in?—and we had all the equipment stowed in Dancer's car. We checked around to ensure we left nothing behind, then got in the car. I sat with my hands squeezing the steering wheel, eyes clamped shut, and breathed deeply.

I have Kane, I told myself, he's safe as long as he's with me. For now. But what about the others? How much do they know about what's happened? My guess was that by now a team would have returned and found the bodies, but I didn't know for sure and information is always useful, so I released my grip, opened my eyes, started the car, and said, "We're making a stop on the way." Then I drove away from the place where we were all supposed to have a happy, carefree week.

The compound was deserted, the vehicles gone. So the doppels knew we'd escaped. Did they know what had happened to Kane? My guess was they'd assume that with everyone dead then Kane was no baby now, but maybe they'd just think it was me. No, they'd know. The bloody hand prints and general carnage would tell them enough, more than enough.

Who'd returned? Just a scout, someone to inform those in charge what had happened?

What was their game-plan? Who was the boss?

Poor Kane. He would never have a remotely normal childhood.

But then, who did? I certainly didn't. Parents that treated me like an interruption to their hedonistic life, never cared for me, became more distant the older I got, that was no normal life. At least Kane was loved and always would be. The rest we'd get through best we could. He wasn't a freak, he was special. He was my son, and that was enough.

"Don't worry, Mother," said Kane as he reached out and wiped my eyes with his soft fingers. "I think I'm going to enjoy my life. So many wondrous things to see and do, so much to learn. So much magic."

"Yes, so much magic."

I wasn't sure if that was a good thing, or a very bad thing.

Urban Jungle

It's astonishing how otherworldly the urban environment looks after spending even just a few days in the splendor of the natural world. As we hit the main arterial road back into the city, I saw everything with new eyes, and sights that usually filled me with happiness for I knew I was back in my city, where I had friends and family, was loved and even a little respected, simply made me depressed. It was unsettling. Even though summer had arrived early, and the sky was cobalt and the fancy office blocks sparkled like the windows had just been washed, much of the city felt drab compared to nature's bountiful offerings.

Streets were grimy, litter tumbled down the roads, buildings appeared cramped, the tenements and terraced houses almost wedged into their narrow plots. City dwellers crammed in like sardines in a can. How did people live like this? How did I? There was a world of open spaces and trees, wild mountains, and clean air just a short drive away, yet many never left the urban environment. Most spent their whole lives in their houses or at their place of work, only ever venturing outside to drive from one to the other.

Was it right, or completely unnatural? Just an extension of the communal cave living of our ancestors I supposed, where families would live in dark places, generations cohabiting on top of one another, so maybe this wasn't so bad after all.

Still, it was depressing, but maybe it was just the mood I was in. After all, I wasn't returning to go home and see my husband and Mithnite, to be given orders by Dancer, not that I ever let him boss me about. No, I was with Kane, and bad men had done bad things to him, and they planned on doing more bad things. I just didn't know what.

The thought of returning to our new home made me feel sick. It wasn't our home yet, not really. The events of the previous year were still too fresh in my mind. The attack, watching our house burn, fearing for my baby and my husband, what I did because of the hate some Hidden felt for me. What would they do to Kane? We had a nice new place, another country cottage with more space than ever and we were making a start on it, slowly easing back into working the land and getting it under control, but I had been little use to be honest, all my time taken up with Kane.

Guess now I could attack it with gusto, have an extra pair of helping hands. But first things first. Get my family back.

I made a decision as we approached the turn to home, and instead I drove into the heart of the city, crawled through rush hour traffic, then entered the maze of side roads that took us deep into the urban jungle. Past corner shops, takeaways, pubs, and wine merchants, the streets narrowed, the terraces getting smaller and smaller. Then we were on a nice tree-lined street, the houses still terraced and insignificant, but the compact front gardens neat, a blaze of bright annual bedding plants and hanging baskets.

I stopped outside a familiar house and turned to Kane. "I don't want any arguments, and please don't make this harder than it already is. It's not safe, and until I know what's happening here, this is the best place for you. Understand?"

"I understand. You worry, you want me to be protected."

I nodded. These were the first words we'd spoken since we entered the city. The brooding atmosphere had affected us both, and I couldn't even imagine how overwhelming it was for him to see such chaos for the first time with if not adult, then certainly not baby eyes. For a start, he could look in all directions, as all he'd known of this world so far was what he'd seen from a baby seat facing the roof of the car. Talk about overexposure.

We got out, I grabbed some bags, figured it best to leave the weapons hidden under blankets as it's not the done thing to tote machine guns in residential Cardiff, and we walked up the short path to a very familiar front door.

As usual, it was unlocked, so I pushed it open and shouted, "It's me, Grandma, and I brought you a visitor."

Tea Time

"Tea's brewing," said Grandma as she popped her head around the open door to the kitchen, then smiled and disappeared.

Feeling apprehensive, and a little nervous if I'm honest, I ushered Kane in and we wandered cautiously into the kitchen.

"Hi, Grandma," I said, holding back the tears.

"Hi, love." Grandma's back was turned to us as she stirred something a worryingly intense shade of orange in a huge pot on the stove. "Hi, Kane," she said like it was the most natural thing in the world.

"Hey, Grandma," he said with a smile.

Then it all got emotional. Grandma put down her spoon, growled at the overworked extractor fan so it sped up hastily, then she smoothed down her apron, put her hands through her hair, and turned to face us with tears in her eyes.

"You're so big," she said as she opened her arms wide and we all rushed to embrace.

A Grandma hug makes everything in the entire world better. It soothes, warms, and comforts, tells you everything will be all right. We hugged tighter than we'd ever hugged, and time swept away. It was just us, just family. This was the real deal. Pure Grandma, no deceit.

Eventually we broke and she said, "Pour the tea, there's a love." So I did.

We all sat at her scrubbed table and took a sip of the strong brew.

"Yum, that's nice," said Kane, eyes twinkling. For some reason I burst out laughing, then so did Grandma. "What's so funny?"

After I'd stopped laughing at the ridiculousness of the situation, I said, "I forgot that you've never had tea before. You're only eight months old."

"He doesn't look it," said Grandma, seemingly taking this all in her stride.

"I'm thirteen, I'm a teenager. That's what it feels like, that's what I am inside and outside. From now on I'll age normally, I can tell. My growth spurt is over."

"Oh, thank God," I gasped, my chest deflating as I let my breath escape. It was such good news. I was dreading him turning into a man, completely missing any of his childhood.

"I knew you were special," said Grandma, taking his hand and squeezing, "but I didn't know this would happen. Okay, I had my suspicions, as your parents are unique, Kane, but something has happened, something bad, I know that much. Only terrible stress could make you change so dramatically. And whatever…" Grandma paused, never let go of his hand, but she glanced away as she thought things through and figured it out. "I see. That makes sense, I suppose. You know what you are now? What this means?"

"I know, Grandma. We would have both been dead otherwise, or Mother would anyway, and I couldn't let that happen. Besides, even before I was born, I knew it was my destiny to become vampire. More, more than just become vampire."

"Just don't get ahead of yourself," warned Grandma, clenching her jaw, trying to look calm but obviously as worried as me. Maybe more so as I didn't know what they were talking about.

"I won't. Plenty of time for all that." Kane smiled and sipped his tea while I was left to make sense of this.

"You're talking about him being Head, aren't you?" My head swam just thinking of it, thinking of him ruling the vampires. "You can't."

"Look, love, he's just a teenager, don't go fretting about that now. And no, I'm not just talking about being the one ruling the local vampires."

"What then?"

"Who knows? But Kane's special. For now, and I want you to listen to me, both of you. For now, just enjoy what you have. The future is long, and mysterious, so don't go worrying about what might be. Think about what you can do to enjoy life and let the future take care of itself."

"Yes, Grandma," said Kane.

"You're right. But I worry."

"And that's as it should be. Parents worry, kids misbehave, that's life."

"Okay."

"Now, let's get down to business." Grandma put aside her tea, stared at both of us long and hard, then asked, "How do you know I'm me? Grandma? I know what's happened, a friendly dwarf filled me in on what Delilah didn't, and bless her, she thinks Kane here is still a baby and that he's at home, but I know the doppels are on the loose, at least the ones you haven't killed, and I'm guessing you both did that?"

We nodded, and I wasn't surprised that she knew the whole story, or that she'd pretended not to know mere moments ago. Witches are worryingly well-informed; it drove Dancer nuts that they always knew his business.

"Okay, so the doppels are at large, and they took Faz and the others, took you but you escaped, so, I ask again, how do you know I'm me?"

"The hug," I said, convinced that however good the doppels were at taking on the appearance, voice, and mannerisms of another, that was one thing they could never accomplish. Fake the love I felt from her hug. The impostor had felt weird when we hugged, Grandma felt perfect.

Grandma smiled. "You're a smart girl. Your mum is a clever lady, Kane, you look after her."

"I will," he said, squaring his shoulders.

"Okay, so, Kate, do you need my help?"

"No, but thanks. You look after Kane, I'll go get them back."

Grandma nodded, she knew this was why we'd come.

"I'm coming with you," said Kane, determined.

"Remember what we spoke about in the car?" Kane grunted; he remembered "Then please do as I ask. Stay here, look after Grandma, don't let anything happen, and I'll sort this mess out. Okay?"

Kane nodded, but he wasn't happy. Tough, sometimes a mother knows best.

Cold

We weren't in the throes of full summer yet, it was still spring really, so although we were getting weird warm days, like mind-bogglingly weird if you knew the Welsh weather, it got cold early, dark too, so it was both of those things when I left Kane in the safe hands of Grandma.

The cold hit like a snowball to the side of the head after the humidity and heat of Grandma's kitchen. I stepped off her threshold and instantly felt alone and estranged from the city I'd called home for so long.

Everything was out of whack, everything was different, everything was more worrying. I'd been stressed ever since Kane was born, knowing he was different and that Hidden would want a piece of him because of it, would be watching him closely to see what happened, had heard the rumors and seen the worshipers, those obsessed with magic and prophecy, but this took it to a whole other level.

I had absolutely no idea what to do. So I went home.

So Strange

Our new place was very different to the last. More impressive, with a large double-bay front, a very cool ancient, battered wooden door that would make any dwarf jealous, chimneys twisted like a witch's finger, clematis and wisteria already scrambling over the dull stone.

The grounds were accessed by a large gate we never closed, as who needed the hassle, and a gravel drive headed straight up to a parking area lined with trees still in their infancy as we'd planted them just weeks after we moved in. We'd kept it lawned at the front, had begun to convert the rear to vegetable gardens and even a small orchard, but there was much to do.

I hardly glanced at the lawn as I drove down the drive and parked. A security light clicked on as I approached, bathing the front of the building and the drive in stark white light, exposing the damp grass. A light fog drifted as the ground cooled and the humidity from the surrounding forest swept through the clearing.

Paranoid, and for good reason, I retrieved the gun from where I'd put it in the passenger-side foot well, and unwrapped it from the blanket. I got out, grabbed a few bags, making sure to pick up the one including everyone's phones, and marched up to the front door. How weird to carry a weapon. I was usually the weapon, and I wondered why I took comfort from this cold lump of metal. Still, I gripped it tight, sorted out the keys, let myself in, closed the door quickly, and leaned against the wood as I breathed deeply.

The house was quiet, and empty, and there hadn't been a single day at this time of the evening when it had been like this. Before we left, I would have been getting Kane ready for bed, changing his nappy, giving him a bath, or putting on his night clothes. Midnite would be grumbling about being hungry, Faz would be either working or joining me helping with Kane, and noise would fill our home.

Now it was silent. And I did not like it one bit.

I wanted my boys back. I wanted to hear laughter and be thinking about bedtime stories. Could I still read to Kane or was he past that already? What about his room? His toys? He didn't even have a bed to sleep in. The nursery was full of baby things. He was a teenager!

My legs went from under me and I slumped to the quarry tiles, not even feeling the cold. All those years, watching him develop, they'd been taken from me, stolen by the doppels for their own sick reasons. They'd done this, they'd robbed me of so much living, so many years, and I could never get them back. Ever.

I was gonna fucking kill them.

Emptiness

I was in a dark place. Both literally and physically.

Lost. Alone. Cold. And afraid.

I didn't know what to do. I didn't know who to trust. I didn't even trust myself.

Look what I'd done to my boy. I'd ruined him in the space of a few months.

"Get a grip, Kate," I whispered into the gloom. "Didn't he just tell you how much he loves being alive? How he feels amazing and is happy to be here? So quit your bitching and get busy."

Not exactly feeling better, but no worse either, I heaved my sorry ass, it was sorry because it was freezing on the quarry tiles, up and flicked on the lights for each room as I passed. In the kitchen I ate what was still fresh in the fridge, and drank coffee. Then I formulated a plan, decided said plan was stupid and would never work, so began again.

Several hours and many cups of coffee later, I got up, washed the dishes, took a shower, set my alarm clock for two hours time, then fell back, naked, onto the bed and was asleep before my head hit the pillow.

When I awoke it was just after midnight, so the room was pitch black. The countryside takes some getting used to as there's no ambient light, no streetlights or cars going past, nothing in the distance lighting up the night sky. All is darkness. All is emptiness.

The house groaned as it settled into its slumber, and I let my hearing expand until it filled the house. I could hear the hobs talking in their fast, strange language, no doubt cleaning up any mess I'd left behind. I was glad I'd put warm milk out for them, even if it was UHT, pleased they'd decided to follow us to the new house, and it made me smile. What a weird, wonderful, dangerous place the Hidden world was.

As I sat up and shivered, welcoming the cold and emptiness, my nakedness and the feel of the new bedding against my pale skin, I smiled.

Who was I kidding? I wouldn't change this for my old life. I'd never go back, even given the chance.

Light on, I dressed, refusing to look closely at the marks still on my flesh from the rope burns, and went downstairs. More coffee, more food, what there was, and with a fresh head, there was more scheming and plotting too.

Mind made up, as many decisions made as were in my power to make actionable, I shouted goodbye to the hobs, called to the emptiness that I may be late coming home in the morning but I'd make it up to them once all this nonsense was over and we were settled back here as a family again, and with a lot of muffled grumbling from the tiny helpers in the shadows, I closed the door and stepped out into the frigid night air.

This was my time, when the vampire came alive. I felt the stirrings of my kind throughout the city, felt them concentrated in one place, Vampire HQ, and as sick as they made me feel, I reached out for them anyway. For their cold, uncaring welcome, the disdain, the downright hostility from many, but they were my kind and I needed the comfort, even if it was just so I knew I wasn't totally alone.

Then I got in the car and I drove back into the city.

I had business to attend to, and I wouldn't be back until it was finished with.

Home to Daddy

For my sins, and trust me, they'd escalated over the last few years, I went to the only place I knew I would be safe. Vampire HQ. It may sound strange, but what safer place when the Hidden Head, the top enforcer, and the deadliest shifter in the city if not the country have been taken by doppels than the heart of vampire territory?

At least there I'd know what was what. Namely, that everyone was a freak and couldn't care less about me as an individual, but would go seriously medieval nasty on anyone or anything that dared even try to hurt one of their own. This is the true dichotomy of the vampire. Most hate each other, not as much as humans, but they have no compassion for their own, would secretly laugh and enjoy the hurt inflicted on other vamps, but it was the principle that mattered. You don't fuck with us. Ever.

So I went to see Oskari.

He was like the father I never had, just not in a good way. My dad was a joke. A lazy, cold, mean, apathetic creature. Oskari was none of those things. He had ambition, was very proactive, and although about as emotional as a brick when it came to love and affection, he was full of other kinds of emotion. Namely, anger and a pathological expectation of respect for his position, his authority, and his sheer vampireness.

HQ was teeming with activity. Everyone was rushing this way and that, the patrols with the vampire Dobermans were moving with intent, more vigilant than usual, cars came and went as I drove through the grounds after waiting an interminable time at the gates to get given the all clear, and as I pulled up to the house things seemed to be bordering on manic.

Without thinking, I grabbed the gun, slung it over my shoulder, and got out of the car.

I didn't stop to ask questions, went straight where I'd been told by the guard. Into the dining room where I usually met Oskari now.

I was ushered in and the door was closed gently behind me by a mean aide I disliked in the extreme—he always reminded me of a vulture with his thin hair and sharp beak of a nose. Plus the talons, a favorite of the elders.

Expecting him to be eating, and maybe offered a seat, I was surprised to find Oskari standing at the head of the empty, polished table. Crossing the floor made me edgy; my heels clicked loudly on the dark wood.

The pictures of his ancestors that lined the walls all seemed to follow me with their disapproving eyes, and I was glad to reach him.

"Oskari, I—"

Oskari's head was bowed as if in thought, his long white hair hanging over his features, but I caught a glimpse of incredible anger as he raised his head then moved faster than I'd believed possible, even for a vampire.

He was behind me, and he pinned my arm up my back, making my shoulder scream, smashed my head so hard into the table that my skull cracked and so did the table, then hissed in my ear, "You really screwed up."

Oskari slammed my head down again, then yanked on my arm and twisted my forearm until the wrist snapped. I screamed as he pounded the broken arm onto the table beside my head, but that didn't satisfy him. He chopped down onto my forearm and pain lanced up as the radius, or ulna, I'm never sure which is which, split like it had been hit with an axe.

"I don't like guns," he hissed as he ripped the machine gun from my shoulder. Then things got really dicey.

As I said, he's like a father to me.

A Deep Hurt

Oskari released me, leaving my head stuck to the table by blood. I watched him side-on from my awkward position as he stepped away, disappeared for a moment, then came back into my line of vision. He smoothed down his black silk shirt, adjusted the cuffs, ran his slender hands through his hair, then put a bloodied finger to his mouth and licked delicately.

"You taste of betrayal," he said, voice so flat, so cold, just like his eyes, that it felt like the worst kind of blow. Not that I wasn't hurting from the damage, but it was as if he'd already dismissed me from his mind, like I was no longer of any importance whatsoever to him. Ancient history, now just a mess to be cleaned up.

"I… I don't understand," I mumbled, finding it hard to speak with my face glued to the table and the fiery lances of pain shooting through my arm and head. I grunted and pushed with my legs to get unstuck, and as I did so the table finally caved in. I collapsed on top of it; blood ran along the wood and dripped onto the expensive Persian rug.

"Don't lie to me," snarled Oskari. "You have betrayed me. Your son is vampire, you made him vampire."

"No, that's not what happened. He made himself vampire, he forced me to, to protect me. To protect himself. He chose."

"Liar!" Oskari hissed like a snake, his eyes dead and predatory. "There were plans, there were things that had to be done first. He should not be vampire. Not now, not yet. You have betrayed us all, ruined our future. All of us are in danger now, all of us are in peril. This is your doing."

I couldn't think straight through the pain. What was he talking about? I took a moment, lying there in a mangled heap on the floor, to focus on the magic and let it surge. It shunted so hard into my arm and head that my muscles spasmed. I screamed as I rolled sideways onto the rug. My arm was locked solid as the wrist snapped back into position. Compounding the pain, the broken bone in my forearm dove under the skin and wriggled about until it found the sweet spot while crazy strong magical forces burrowed through the already reconfiguring nerves until I managed to control the flow and make it smooth and steady.

My head buzzed as tiny fractures healed and burst capillaries and blood vessels were cauterized then connected together again, giving me a blinding headache that left me almost unconscious. But I wouldn't lose it now, had to remain alert, as this was far from over.

This entire episode took but several seconds, so by the time I'd finished hitting the ground and rolling away from the table my bones were already repairing. My heart remained broken though.

I should have known better. I did know better. Oskari had no love for me. Sure, I was valuable to him, a strong, strange vampire that had grown to immense power and status over the years. From a scared, reticent woman to something unique, and with Kane I was probably the most valuable piece of meat in the country, maybe the world.

He had me. He had plans. He wanted to use me.

Well, I was over being used. I put a stop to that years ago. He wanted to use my son, he wanted to make him vampire but on his terms, when he was ready.

Thoughts flashed through my mind as I finished my roll. He wanted to manipulate Kane, to turn him into something dark and dangerous, to use him to fight for his own ends and that of the vampires. But there was more. Something else. Something I hadn't even considered.

I sprang, cat-like, to my feet, refusing to be a victim, refusing to be treated like this.

"Who the fuck do you think you are?" I spat, knowing I'd been warned about ever talking to Oskari this way.

"I'm your Head. I own you."

"Nobody owns me. Not you, not Faz, not anyone. You think I'm scared? Maybe, but that doesn't mean you can abuse me. I've had abusers in the past, never again. You want to use my son, you want to turn him into something despicable, something cold and uncaring like you? I won't allow it." I put my hands on my hips and stared down the most powerful vampire in the country, refusing to look away.

Oskari laughed. "Haha. You are such a simple creature. You have no concept of the pain I can inflict on you. But you will find out. I will have the boy. It's not too late to salvage this mess you have made. You let him become vampire before his time, before he was ready. Before I was ready. Still, I may be able to show him the way, teach him."

"You're scared of him," I said, suddenly understanding exactly why Oskari was so incensed. "You're afraid of my son. You didn't want him turned until you'd filled his head with your crap so he wouldn't be a threat to you. You. Are. Scared."

Oskari didn't flinch, but I saw him swallow hard, saw the slight tic at his cheek, and I knew I was right. He was scared because he knew the power Kane would have, did have, and knew that given time Kane would threaten his position. More, threaten the entire vampire way of life, the vampires themselves. Why? Because he was my son and I would rather die than let him ever become cold like the others, like Oskari. I would instill virtue and understanding in him from my own somewhat warped perspective. But he would always have love and compassion, never look at humans as cattle, or in any way inferior.

"You wanted to take him from me and use him for your own gain. To become like you but under your control."

"Of course. He's a valuable addition to our family, to my Ward. He is a child with Hidden magic, born of vampire. It was clear he would be unique, but with your rapid pregnancy and his obvious awareness of his surroundings, which you overlooked, it became apparent he would develop fast. Now you've ruined it. They've ruined it."

I went hot, then cold, then hot again.

"You planned this didn't you? You took Faz and the others, had the doppels take Kane and me. What, to keep us separate from them? To control us?"

"They betrayed me, just as you have done. They were to bring you both back safe and sound, let you escape, let you return to me, your family. But they wanted him for their own, made you change him, made him change himself. It was too soon, they betrayed me," he said again, almost a whisper, and then I finally understood all that had happened.

"You bastard! What, I was to come home, think everything was all right? Ah, the doppels were to replace Faz and Dancer, take their place with some pretend fight or something so I'd think they'd won and the doppels were beaten. My God what is wrong with you?"

"I would have been in control, had people in place to run this country, control all Hidden. You all betrayed me," screamed Oskari.

Then things got serious.

A Big Fight

"Where are they?" I shouted. Everything felt out of whack. I watched, mesmerized for a moment, as spittle caught the light cast by the numerous lamps, tiny particles of hate directed at Oskari. They twinkled like flailing stars as they traversed the void, and one tiny, almost imperceptible speck landed on Oskari's pale, flawless cheek.

It sent him apoplectic with rage.

"Taken, being meticulously copied as instructed, no doubt. But the doppels overstep the boundaries, same as you. They've deceived me, want to assume the positions for themselves. They will use Kane."

"Like you want to. You deserve this, you are the one who has betrayed. You betrayed me, your own kind. You're just a manipulator like the rest."

"Enough!" Two spots of color darkened Oskari's cheeks and he wiped at the spittle that kept flying. Somehow we were mere feet apart now, like he'd moved without me noticing. The failure of his plan and the realization nothing was going as he'd wanted seemed to consume him.

My son, my baby boy, was feared by the likes of Oskari, and that scared me, truly it did. What was to become of him? What now? Oskari would kill him, I felt it in my bones. If his plan to have those under his control assume Dancer's position and to use Kane to do his bidding had been ruined, then Kane was a danger to him.

I had to get to him, protect him. The others too. Oskari would eradicate them all, including the doppels. The doppels themselves would be trying to mimic them exactly and the moment their studies were over they'd kill them.

It was a race to get them first, so I'd better get going.

Just one slight problem.

Oskari punched at me, and in my dazed and confused state I was slow to react. His fist hit me square on the nose—yes, my nose again—and it not so much broke as shattered then splatted across my face. The force whipped my head back, almost breaking my spine, and as it rebounded forward the muscles strained then snapped, sending me flying across the room and hammering into the wall. I slumped to the floor and sat there, head lolling to the side, the muscles ruined, my face broken, bloodied, and bruised. I held in my screams.

I wouldn't give him the satisfaction.

I pushed with my hands to get to my feet but Oskari was already on me. He snarled and punched out again and again, pulverizing my face, smashing bone to pulp, and as my eyes swelled up until I couldn't see, I felt his fierce, cold breath on my face before the beating stopped.

I heard him step away and shout, "Bring me food," and then there was a scuffling and the sound of doors opening and closing.

As the swelling eased a little, I made out a blurry outline of a naked young woman trembling before Oskari. He grabbed her hair, bent her head, and sank his teeth into her neck. In seconds she was little but a dried up husk; he let the body fall to the floor.

His head tilted back and he gasped loudly.

"Now, let's give you your punishment, shall we?" he said, moaning in ecstasy, voice full of passion. Oskari's eyes turned red as the blood magic coursed through his veins and his strength increased a thousand-fold.

"Maybe make me go without my dinner? Send me to my room?" I gasped.

Oskari sneered then launched himself at me.

No Chance

To someone observing this scene, I was like a helpless child. Beaten, defeated, cowering on the floor before the almost Godlike presence of her overbearing, abusive father.

Been there, done that, not going back thank you very much. Whatever he did, I would not go out like that. I would not shy away from confrontation, I would not be made to feel bad or inferior, made to believe I was somehow in the wrong as my elders always knew better. I've experienced enough to know that just because someone is older, it doesn't make them smarter or always right. All it does is make them older, and often more closed-minded and insular than someone younger.

Well, Oskari was ancient, certainly set in his ways, and believed utterly in his own sense of rightness. A megalomaniac, like most vampires, especially all vampire Heads if the stories are true.

But above all that, above my refusal to allow him to dominate and belittle me, to treat me like a naughty girl, was my refusal to leave behind my family, my life, my existence.

I took the first punch right to the face without trying to move. As his bloodied fist came straight at me again, and this time he and I both knew it would split my head wide open and that would be the end of me, I let the raw, but now rejuvenated muscle in my neck spring back like an elastic band.

Faster than his fist—and trust me it was fast—my head whipped to the side and he punched the wall, obliterating plaster and the brick behind, raining down dust on my shoulder.

"Haha, getting slow in your old age," I taunted, blood dripping from my fat, split lip, my bruised face healing so I could finally see again.

It's hard to explain how rapidly this all happened. Thoughts were formed as fast as I could run, all movements a blur to the Regular eye. Full on vamp fight in other words.

"Bitch," he spat, and punched faster and harder.

Each blow was dodged as my head weaved, and all the while I was getting to my feet until I had my back against the wall, dodging his assault easily as Hidden magic, something he could never have, consumed me.

I shot out an arm with speed that surprised Oskari but not me. He didn't know me, he didn't know what I was capable of under extreme duress, and this was about as extreme as it got. The life and future of everyone I cared about was on the line, and I would not let him win.

He was shunted back ten feet as my fist made contact with his chest, the ribs cracking, the breastbone splitting. His eyes widened and then he grinned, like he was pleased I was more of a match than he'd expected.

"Good, very good."

"You were going to use my baby. I'll destroy you, take everything from you," I screamed, a bit over-excited and maybe somewhat dramatic because of it, but I think it's understandable.

"You're a baby yourself, a child. You cannot defeat me, ever." Oskari was at me before the last word hit my ears, his hands at my throat. The momentum carried us both to the opposite wall. He squeezed, fingers locked tight around my throat, the death grip of the vampire.

"Wanna bet." Magic swarmed through the ink that fattened and sent pure, violent energy up from the intricate patterns just below my collar line. It engorged my neck, and his hands flew apart as fiery red sparks erupted.

He gasped as he held out his hands, the skin blistering and the magic wrapping around him like a million strands of silk as it grew tighter, binding his hands together. The heat grew more intense as my focus increased and dismay and anger spilled over, until they were on fire. The flesh melted away like butter in a pan.

He snarled, the tendons in his neck standing out as he used his immense strength to pull his hands apart.

The magic flew off in all directions, dissipating as it went. His skeletal hands, blackened muscle and bone exposed, healed even as I launched forward and feinted low then stabbed out right into his goddamn pale eyes, bloodshot from magic. One eyeball popped warm liquid over my fingers and I ripped his nose with the other, yanking away flesh and cartilage.

He stumbled back and I fell with him, never letting go, pushing my finger deeper into the eye socket, searching for his brain so I could squish it to mush.

Something hammered over my back, like getting hit by a troll, and I turned to see an entire section of the table arcing toward me, the aide who'd ushered me in swinging with grim determination.

It cracked over my head and I was thrown off Oskari as everything went black.

I was in big trouble.

New Enemies

Vampires aren't nice people, although ask a vampire and they'd say they weren't a nice vampire—being called a person seen as an insult worthy of them doing something nasty like biting your face off and stuffing it down any handy holes they made. What I naively hadn't realized until now was quite how not nice some vampires can be. Sure, I knew their nature was frosty verging on glacial, and that the suffering of others didn't affect them, that taking a life was seen as a right, nothing to worry over, about as stressful and guilt-inducing as eating an egg, but it still hadn't quite sunk in what the normal attitude of my brethren was.

I found out, boy did I find out.

While I was semi-conscious, Oskari ordered the aide to bind me with a strange thin wire around my hands and feet, a material I'd heard talk of but never seen before. This was becoming a worrying habit. Not satisfied, it was wrapped around my neck and then my upper arms and thighs too. I felt this was overkill but was in no position to argue. It appeared delicate, like gossamer, but was razor sharp, and any movement made it cut deep into my flesh. There was no getting out of it if you wanted to keep your hands and feet, and personally I quite like them. It aids with mobility.

Once trussed up like a fly in a spider's web, I had my clothes cut from me, leaving me naked and standing in the middle of Oskari's dining room dripping blood over the polished floor. That'd teach him.

The two men spoke for several minutes out of earshot then a hatch slid aside in the dark paneled wall and a very modern bank of electronic equipment activated. Buttons were pressed and then the ceiling made a strange whirring sound, although it was hard to see as my eyesight was still bad and craning my neck hurt too much. Plus, the wire, and the last thing I wanted was to chop my head off. That would not end well.

Not to worry, as soon enough I got to see the surprise. A cross, simple yet beautiful in design, made of blond ash and polished until it gleamed, descended from the ceiling, hanging from thick steel cable. They wouldn't, would they?

What were they going to do, crucify me? I chuckled, thinking it ridiculous, that this was just an elaborate way of making miscreants tow the line, but then I thought about how steeped in tradition the vampire culture is, how old Oskari was, and that no matter how anti-religion the current vampires were, the old ones had religious traditions and iconography etched into their very being. They'd lived through periods of history when belief was at the heart of everything everyone did. When archaic, barbarous acts were performed on the disbelievers, when vampires were burned at the stake, tortured to make them confess they were in cahoots with the Devil.

Oskari was old skool all the way. He was ruthless, efficient, ran the UK vampires with an iron fist the likes of which no previous Head had ever managed, and took unkindly to anyone challenging his authority.

I'd ruined his plans, turned Kane vampire before he had chance to indoctrinate my son, had kept Kane apart from him, left him with Grandma, all of which was far from what Oskari had in mind for this epic subterfuge. But worse than all that, more deserving of punishment, was that I'd defied him to his face. I'd fought back, cursed him out, even laid my hands on him. Heck, I'd taken his damn eye, which looking at him from where I stood, seemed futile and a rather rash thing to do. His eye was back, his skin was flawless, he was right now brushing his lustrous hair, and had already cleaned himself up and dressed in fresh clothes. He looked like nothing had happened.

And here I was. Naked, broken bones still repairing, covered in blood—mine and his—hurting on so many levels the physical seemed almost inconsequential, and staring at a bloody cross in a spooky dining room.

"Gather the others," Oskari ordered the aide. He scowled in my direction before leaving me alone.

I sagged once I knew the room was empty. I wouldn't give him the satisfaction of seeing me anything but defiant, but I was very scared.

My world had been well and truly turned on its head. Deep down, I knew what Oskari was, but I'd been drawn to him, felt a bond, a deep connection. It's my own fault. I was looking for something I should have known I'd never have. A father who loved and cared for me. All I got was more of the same. A man who thought of me as nothing but a way for him to get what he wanted.

Oskari had used me for years, I knew and understood that, it was part of the way all Heads operated. Every action was considered, the big picture always in mind. Even Dancer thought and acted on information I wasn't privy too, but stupid as it sounds, I trusted Oskari. I believed I knew him, even understood him a little, that he had a moral code even though he was Head.

I was wrong, so very wrong. Utterly naive. He'd set up this elaborate plan so he could get Dancer, Faz, Persimmon, even Mithnite cloned, basically leaving him in control of the country, and able to influence and order the main players in the human Hidden world. And he'd done it in such a way that would lead to Kane and I being taken then escaping, coming to him for help maybe, leaving me and my boy at the mercy of him and the doppels.

They would have played us, slowly turned me into something despicable, influenced my child's upbringing then used Kane to cement his hold over the human Hidden of not just the country but probably the world. Wield Kane like a weapon, the most powerful human there had been in maybe centuries, maybe ever. No other human as far as I knew had ever been able to shape-shift, do what the doppels did, wield magic, and be a vampire. It was unheard of, but Oskari had known he would possess such abilities, or had hoped at the least, and now his dreams were if not shattered then certainly cracked.

He'd do whatever it took to get things back on track, and that meant getting Kane and eliminating me. He'd also be after the doppels, would eradicate them for their treachery. Which, I suddenly realized, meant there would be no clones of the others put into place, and he could never let them go free.

At the first opportunity, Oskari would annihilate the doppels, murder the Head, kill Persimmon, Mithnite, and Faz, and then, once he had Kane, he'd destroy me and do his best to control my son and make him do his bidding.

If it was the last thing I did before I died, I'd drag Oskari right down to hell with me.

"Bring it on, you bitch," I said, just not too loud in case he heard.

Beyond Expectations

I'd tried to be good, I really had. I'd kept out of trouble, stayed away from Hidden politics, refrained from taking any enforcer jobs, just looked after Kane and kept my head down. It hadn't worked. What was meant to be a nice vacation had turned into a nightmare on an epic scale, way beyond anything I'd ever dealt with in my role as enforcer.

This was the life I'd chosen, and once you're in you can't get out. My family was too deeply entrenched in all things Hidden for me to ever escape this and live a life that was even semi ordinary.

As I stood naked and bleeding, I understood with every fiber of my being that this was a turning point for me and mine. After this night, if I survived, there would be no going back. Our lives would be transformed and nothing would ever be the same again.

There would be no happy families, no peaceful weekends at home, digging the veg plots, having a superficially Regular life, switching off from the outside world for days or weeks at a time. This was it, the crux, the point of no return. Kane was too special, and we had too much focus on us as individuals and as a family, for us to play at being normal.

I think that scared me more than anything else, even more than the terrible trouble we were presently in. That even if we squirmed out of this utter mess it wouldn't bring peace and isolation, give us freedom and more choices. We'd be more boxed in than ever, more caught up in the world of the Hidden, trapped in madness with no chance of ever extracting ourselves from the murderous power plays and machinations of the higher echelons. We'd be those people, up to our eyeballs and responsible not just for our own safety but for countless beings who looked to us for guidance.

For this could only end one way, and that was for me to eliminate our enemies.

All of this imbued me with a deep, soul-crushing sense of sadness. We'd be thrust into the Hidden limelight whether we wanted to or not. Kane would be at the center of it all, forever marked as a man apart. Yet, there was something else, something I didn't want to admit but knew now was the time to do so.

I wouldn't change a thing.

To hold this kind of power, to be something unique and special, is intoxicating and utterly addictive. To play with the elemental forces of the universe is a rare and wondrous gift, and the things I'd felt, the things I'd done, they were a true blessing. If I were religious then I would call it a gift from God, although I knew many thought of it as the Devil's curse. But, as usual, this was all mankind's doing.

And above all this, above thoughts of the future and the uncertainty it would bring no matter the outcome of this current problem, this pressing, very immediate danger that threatened our happiness and very existence, was the concern of a mother.

If for no other reason than to ensure my son survived, I would do all I could to get out of this. To protect him, nurture him, teach him the right way to be responsible and become a man deserving of respect. I just had to get away, and as I looked up and the door opened, that was looking less and less likely.

Vampires young and old filed into the large dining room, each and every one of them serious, faces somber. But I caught the sneers, the twinkling eyes of expectation, the bloodlust rising in anticipation. I saw the hatred. There were even a few sorrowful and scared faces of friends, or as close to friends as they could ever be in this world.

I was grabbed from behind, the bindings tearing into flesh that couldn't repair properly because the cuts went so deep, and then I found myself positioned on the cross, arms out to the sides, limbs tied tight.

This was an archaic ritual, older than Christianity itself, and I knew all about it. All vampires did. This was the ultimate punishment for those who betrayed everything being a vampire stood for.

Crucifixion by committee.

Blood dripped from my hands and feet as wire chewed deep until it was grinding against bone. I stared at the single long steel nail every vampire held in front of them like an offering to the gods.

Oskari entered wearing full white ceremonial robes, his pale hair brushed until it shone, his eyes hidden behind his dark, gold-rimmed sunglasses, making him look like a rapper bishop.

I laughed at the image it conjured, but when he drew his arms forward to reveal the hammer, my laugh turned to a choke.

Broken Ties

"…betrayed her family."

I began humming to myself the moment I saw the hammer, so missed most of the crap Oskari spouted. I didn't want to listen, knew it would rile me up and make me stress more when I had to do something different. I had to take myself off to another place, get away from my body and the damage about to be inflicted. So I hummed a lullaby and zoned out, but came back for Oskari's dramatic finale.

He turned to face me, the room now packed with eager vampires. He lifted the hammer and showed me a gleaming seven inch nail sharper than his teeth. Trust me, his teeth were plenty sharp.

Oskari removed his sunglasses and gave them to the damn aide. The Head approached, then placed the nail against my open right palm. The crowd's eyes snapped to black. They hissed as hundreds of incisors snicked down. The most terrifying sound I have heard in my life apart from the screams of Kane as he died in the dirt.

Oskari whirled three-sixty, the utter knob, and with a single blow from the hammer he crucified me.

The aide went next. Then, one by one, while I hummed, giving them no satisfaction, the rest took their turn. I stared at Oskari the whole time—even though I was far away and focusing on singing to Kane as a baby in his cot while he smilcd and squirmed and made cooing noises—as the vampires each hammered a nail into my body so it pierced flesh and bone and pinned me to the wooden cross.

I lost consciousness many times throughout the hours-long ordeal, but every time I came back from the beautiful oblivion I locked eyes with Oskari and I hummed the lullaby. He remained stationed in front of me the whole time, stoically watching, passing the hammer back and forth, each vampire handing it to him after they'd finished.

The hammer grew bloodier and bloodier until it was so slick that Oskari called for a cloth. Once wiped, he handed it with grim detachment to the next vampire, one who I'd had several run-ins with because he was a dick and I was brilliant.

This guy, Randal, took the hammer and smirked at me. He approached, whispered, "Bitch," then placed the nail on my kneecap and whacked the head. Pain exploded through my body the likes of which I hadn't thought possible, then I was back in the nursery singing to Kane and merely experiencing the torment from a distance.

Then Randal hit the nail again and this time his curse of, "Mother of monsters," echoed around the room.

The room went deathly silent as Randal stepped back, his face twitching and sweat beading instantly on his head as he understood what he'd done. This torment may have been barbaric, and in their eyes deserved, but you didn't go around calling vampires names, especially ones whose child Oskari held in the utmost regard and saw as part of the destiny of our entire kind. Randal had insulted Oskari. He could have called me names, although he would have been severely reprimanded, but this was a step too far.

"Hold him," ordered Oskari.

Randal panicked and tried to fight them off, even did a good job for a minute or two, but they got him eventually, held him fast as he pleaded and cried, shaming himself. Oskari was handed a nail and with vampire swiftness he slammed the nail into Randal's forehead then drove it home with a gentle tap of the hammer.

Randal dropped down dead. Oskari looked back at me and said, "I apologize for the insult," then handed the hammer to the next in line as Randal's body was dragged away.

The crucifixion continued, each nail hurting more no matter how hard I tried to remain a thing apart. Magic surged and did its best to repair me, some of the nails even pushing out from the wood and flesh so wounds could heal, but each nail drained me further. My body couldn't fix itself with these things stuck through me, and my injuries became life-threatening.

It was my sanity I was more concerned about.

I think I began to cackle and then laugh, maybe even sob a little, but every time I found myself doing it I came back to the lullaby, and I never once gave Oskari the satisfaction of looking away or begging. I stared at him throughout the whole ordeal, which must have taken most of the night.

The final vampire stepped forward, drove a nail through my forearm as there was nowhere else left to do it, such a pin-cushion had I become, and then all the vampires, with Oskari at the fore, stood and stared at me.

Oskari's white robes were drenched in blood from repeatedly handling the hammer and from the spurts that hit him as the nails hit arteries that thankfully healed by taking a slightly circuitous route around the foreign body. The floor was slick with my blood which had caused several of them to slip and fall over, giving me at least something to laugh at amid the horror.

"Soon you will die. We shall leave you in peace while the life ebbs from your broken body. Rest assured, I shall look after your son. He will be a credit to us all." Oskari bowed to me formally, and I spat at him. I spat at them all.

"You're all going to die. Every last one of you," I warned, and I saw it in his eyes. He was scared. They all were.

And for good reason. Nobody survived this, nobody. Nobody ever had, and I think we were all amazed I'd lasted as long as I had. I know I was. But I wasn't just vampire, and they were worried.

"The ritual is done. Leave," ordered Oskari.

I can't for the life of me think why he didn't end me then. Maybe it was a grudging respect for what I'd endured. Maybe he felt compelled to stick to the ritual.

Maybe he was too scared.

It Gets Worse

It must have been early morning because I could hear birds singing. It brought a smile to my face, flesh thankfully not pierced by a nail. In fact, my whole head was undamaged, along with all vital organs. This was a slow death, bringing me from the heights of magic and vampire power down to the level of a Regular so I'd bleed out during the day.

I wasn't strong enough to battle this any longer. My magic had done what it could but it wasn't enough to repair the damage that got worse as my system devoured itself searching for energy to heal the myriad wounds. Each nail felt red raw, blistered and terribly hot as magic attempted to defend against the foreign bodies. To heal muscle and knit bone back together. It was a losing battle, but my system worked away in the background nonetheless to do what could be done.

It was failing.

I was still vampire but had little of the strength and vitality that made us so superhuman. My defenses were down; I was little more than a normal person now. Even my ink had receded, hardly fattened at all, the magic swimming through the patterns lethargic and backing up as it encountered the damage it found impossible to bypass.

The birds sang louder, which made me happy. I wondered how I could hear them in such a room, protected as it was from the outside world, the heavy wooden shutters normally blocking out most sound. I glanced up and saw a young vampire open up the last shutter then leave without even looking my way. Ah, so that was it. The the blinds had been pulled, so early morning light could stream into the room as the sun rose.

That would be nice, to die as the sun bathed me in its warmth, its goodness, its pure brilliance and beauty.

I spent some time listening to the birds and my own raspy breathing, watched, mesmerized as motes danced in rays of sunlight angling through the window as the sun peeked above the hills beyond. Strong shafts of wholesome light lit the floor like white fire, as if to sear away my pain and everything bad in the world. I watched as one slowly moved, then more appeared as the sun rose properly, until the room was awash with brush strokes of palest purity.

The room emerged from the shadows, ninja-style, and with it came a tingling all over. Nothing noteworthy at first, just a strange sensation I'd never experienced before. Then it grew more intense, then it hurt, even through the torture I was already experiencing, and then a single ray of light hit my thigh.

Flesh split instantly, actually burst into flame, and oh boy the agony of such a thing. It made everything else pale into insignificance, truly it did. The sun hitting my skin was suffering of the purest, most base kind, and it seared my soul until I could stand it no longer.

But stand it I did, for I had no choice.

More light bathed the room, until suddenly the whole interior was bright and stark, darkness banished, replaced with light like the scene had been washed over with watercolors, everything transparent and faint. But that may have just been my tears.

I began to burn in earnest. Flesh steamed, then hissed, bubbled and popped. Blisters grew massive then oozed. Streaks of red destroyed my skin, sections burst into flame, and the intensity heightened until I knew the end had come.

When I regained consciousness it was to discover that first, I was still alive, and second, I wasn't burning. It was more like a gentle simmer, just beneath the boiling point, but enough to roast me alive like I was slow cooked meat.

This was my true punishment.

I was so debilitated, so weak, with so little left of my vampire nature that I had nothing in me to fight the one thing all vampires avoided eventually.

The sun.

It was cooking me. The defenses all young vampires have for many years had been stripped from me along with everything else. Thankfully, the sun was high now, so there wasn't as much direct light, and the room was gloomy again, but it still burned, still roasted me alive.

Come dusk, when the dying rays of the sun brightened the room through the west windows, it would kill me, of that I had no doubt.

I laughed, as you had to see the funny side of it. Here I was, a vampire who had fought her nature every step of the way, and I would die in the one way I'd never even considered.

I had the rest of the day, then I was toast. Crispy, burned toast.

A Long Wait

I couldn't focus, couldn't escape to dreams and lullabies, was consumed by the daylight until all else faded to nothing. I hardly even thought of my family, couldn't get my brain to function, as though the sun took even that away from me. I knew it was my wounds getting worse, that I was adrift on a sea of broken bones and frayed veins, helpless and stranded on a raft of pure pain. My body had almost given up, was fighting to survive, the magic having done its best but not up to the task.

My body burned from the daylight and from infection that tore at my system, flaying my flesh and exposing my shivering, then burning, then sweating, then spasming body to degrees of torture unimaginable.

But, and you should be proud, I did not call for help. None would come, just Oskari to gloat. I knew he was awake, sensed his presence along with all the other vampires. They were waiting for me to ask for forgiveness, expecting it. To plead for mercy, beg to be released from this hell. I would not. I knew they'd never release me, would just smile their smug smiles. It was what Oskari wanted, to see me brought down to something base, and the longer I held out the more agitated he became. I felt his unease and that gave me strength enough to see this through to the end.

It was coming soon, I knew, and as the afternoon drew on and I became hardly alive at all, I felt Oskari finally retire, his mind quieten. There was no smug satisfaction from him, just the knowledge of duty performed, of him continuing the work of his kind. The others retreated too, the few left that hadn't already succumbed to the sleep of the damned.

I was already dismissed, a brief part of Oskari's long history. A mere blip, of no import now I had been punished. His focus had already shifted; he was looking to the future. He would be after Kane when he arose this night, may already have put plans into action to retrieve him. There was no turning back for him now.

What he'd done meant the wrath of Grandma and thus all witches, and that was a serious declaration of war. If anyone ever found out of course. Then it hit me, even in my befuddled state. Nobody knew I was here, nobody would ever know what had happened. Everyone would think my fate had been the same as Faz's. That's what Grandma would think. That the doppels had done this, leaving Oskari in the clear for his murderous machinations.

What about Kane? Would he figure it out? Yes, at some point he would. Being vampire meant he would have access to the communal mind, and one day, when he was mature, maybe a slip of the tongue, maybe sensing something in the minds of the others, he would know. But by then it might be too late for him to act, or maybe he'd be so warped by Oskari that he wouldn't seek revenge. Did I want him to?

I let such concerns drift away. I was helpless, could do nothing to change the future. I just had to have faith in my son that he would remain a good boy and would lead a righteous life. One without parents.

More than anything else that had happened, that made me the angriest. To grow up without parents, for that I could never forgive Oskari.

Thoughts became muddled, I was lost to fever and delirium, my world one of pain and suffering. I couldn't focus on anything, couldn't keep my thoughts straight, and I began to see things.

The room wobbled, the walls, floor, and ceiling bowing in then expanding out to fill the universe. The air took on magical colors of the rainbow, reality whirling and dancing until it made me dizzy. Everything was shutting down. At one point I even thought I saw a head pop up through the floor before I shook violently and when I looked again it was gone.

Hours drifted by, the day lasting an eternity but time still going by too fast as this was to be my last few hours of life. When the sun dropped low in the clear blue sky on a perfect day I would burn and I would turn to dust.

I had but one regret. I wouldn't see my son mature into a man.

The Evening Comes

I woke with a start, my body convulsing. Incredible pain engulfed me and I gasped and cried out but stifled the scream because I refused to let anyone hear me suffer, to get any more enjoyment from my misery.

The room was brighter, my skin was blistering and smoking, and I knew time was almost up. There was a thick, shiny pool of blood spread out at my feet now, more blood than I'd imagined could be contained within a human body. It was dark, almost black, drying up, not enough left for me to bleed much more now. I guess the faint traces of magic remaining were enough to stop me dying. It was kind of annoying. It would have been better to have lost consciousness and never woken up, rather than have to be a witness to my own nasty death.

I mean, come on, like I hadn't been through enough already.

The curse of the Hidden. Sometimes magic's great, other times it can be the last thing you want. The shafts of yellow afternoon sunlight traced across the floor, and would hit my flesh soon enough. Already I was beginning to fry in weak spots on my body, of which there were many, and the wounds around the nails began to crisp up then smolder. Soon they would burst into flames and I would be consumed.

I began to hallucinate again, saw that damn head appear out of the floor, rising like Death had come to take me. Maybe he had. Maybe this was what happened when you died and Death really did make an appearance. A smile spread, and I spoke as loud as I could, the words coming out as nothing but a faint whisper. "Hello, Death, you took your time."

The head emerged, nothing but a shadow with the sun as a backdrop, and then there were a pair of shoulders, then arms, then torso, and then the Grim Reaper himself stood before me. Time to say goodbye.

"Where's your scythe?" I asked.

Death put a hand to his face and scratched, then said, "Huh?"

Which was odd. Surely he'd say something more menacing, some epic final words or something? And where was his billowing cloak, and why were his arms so long? If anything, he looked more like the Chemist than the bloke that took you to meet your maker.

"Chemist?" I asked, confused and wondering if any of this was real.

"Yes, it's me," whispered the Chemist, glancing around then hurrying over.

"You're not Death are you?" I asked, watching a shaft of light reach the pool of blood. It smoked, burst into flame, then died. Talk about symbolism you could do without.

"What? Eh? No, I've come to rescue you."

"Oh, that's nice," I said, thinking it would have been even nicer if he'd come before the bit with the crucifixion. Still, it was a kind gesture, but he'd never get me down, never save me.

"Hold still," he said, as he pulled a vial from his checkered shirt pocket and removed the cork with his rotten teeth.

"Haha. Oh, that's a good one," I cackled.

He looked confused for a moment, then grinned, his green, jagged teeth the most welcome sight I'd ever seen. His melted face, his patchy hair, his deformed body so beautiful as it was the body of a friend. "Open wide."

I opened my mouth, the skin ripping on my lips, and he poured a black liquid onto my tongue. I swallowed.

The pain of this potion made the crucifixion seem like a nice way to go out. It burned, itched, seared, and consumed me from the inside out. It did not, in any way, make me feel better. I was being tortured to the last, would die in more pain than I'd believed possible, and I'd already thought I'd reached the pinnacle of what the human body could endure.

The sun traced across the bloody pool the Chemist was standing in, and he looked at it nervously. "Come on, come on," he said, tapping his foot, splashing my own life force.

Something pinged and he smiled, then again, and again, and again. Nails dropped into the blood, splashing or thudding against the floor, and then more, and more, and more, popping from the wood, reversing the direction they had taken and exiting my body.

The nail in my kneecap came loose with a nasty crunch, then in unison the final two burst from my palms. The wire unwound, and I fell forward into the Chemist's arms. He wrapped me up in them tight, and hurried away from the light, then lay me on the floor.

"You won't like this next bit," he said with a frown of concern I found hilarious.

As I laughed, he poured something else into my mouth and I coughed and spluttered then swallowed.

The world became different, as if I was lying on a delicate membrane that was a barrier between one world and another. The Chemist took my hand in his and we fell through the floor into madness.

Mistaken Identity

Maybe I was hallucinating and this was Death, and he'd taken on the form of a familiar face to ease the transition from one plane to the next. It certainly felt like I'd died. And not in a good way.

Pain was compounded by the potions the Chemist had given me, which I understood may have merely been symbolic, a way for me to cope with what was happening. Every wound on my body felt like it was tightening up and scabbing over simultaneously, the sheer deep itch enough to drive me insane. The liquid hitting my stomach burned like acid, and I felt it spread through my ink like it could activate it.

Was this the magic gathering itself before it returned to the Empty at my death? A precursor to my soul's release?

Darkness enveloped me, the chattering sounds of the creatures of the earth insinuated their way into my mind until I wanted to scream, but thought maybe that would mean a mouth full of dirt or nasty beasties.

I was descending into hell, traveling through the bowels of the earth into the dark, nasty places reserved for the truly wicked. I hadn't been that bad, had I? Hadn't I tried to do the right thing? Maybe it wasn't enough. Maybe I was evil and this was my due.

On and on it went, traversing limbo where all was black, occupied by a cacophony of creatures feeding on the rotten epicenter of my soul, scratching and clawing and feasting on my putrid innards.

Light broke, somehow familiar and comforting, and I realized I was being dragged by the Chemist. My other arm came free and I clawed at a swirling pattern, unable to register its significance. Then another hand reached out and grabbed mine and I was yanked from purgatory.

With a thud, I landed sideways and stared at a pair of pink fluffy slippers leading up to wrinkled tights. The patterns coalesced and I understood this was a familiar carpet in a room that hadn't changed in decades.

I rolled onto my back and stared into concerned eyes.

"Grandma?"

"Hush, love. It's okay, you're safe now."

I smiled. I screamed so loud and violently that Grandma's tears soaked my face as they fell. But I didn't die.

Let's Try Again

Two more faces peered down at me. The Chemist and Kane.

"Th… thank you," I stuttered, meaning it with all my heart.

"You're welcome," beamed the Chemist. "I got to make potions with Grandma. I knew we could save you."

"How? How did you know?" I asked, even though my tongue was twice its normal size and my lips were oozing something they definitely ought not to, wanting an answer to at least something.

"I sensed your pain, Mother. I thought my godfather would have the best chance of saving you. But they will pay." Kane's demeanor changed then, and I wouldn't have wanted to be standing opposite him when he got really angry.

"They will. Um, I kinda screwed up, guys. Next time I'll do better."

"Next time you'll have us with you," said Grandma, face set in that determined way that tells you there's no questioning her decision or her authority.

Kane and the Chemist nodded and I didn't have the energy to argue. I couldn't even remain conscious.

A Brief Respite

From the dark depths of my dreams something nagged at me, and I struggled to consciousness even though I knew it would be to a world of pain and despicable humanity. I fought through the bliss of unknowingness and emerged a creature born of fire.

I was running hot, the fever consuming me, but I wasn't nailed to a cross so as far as I was concerned things were on the up. Grandma's sofa was so comfortable I could have stayed there for a lifetime, but there was work to be done, family to save, and I didn't have a moment to spare. We had to get the others safe before the doppels destroyed them and tried to take their place, if it wasn't already too late.

I opened my eyes and was taken aback to find I was wearing one of Grandma's peculiar nighties. A thick pink flannel thing with lace at the hems—attractive it was not. Still, it was better than being naked. Just.

"Eat," ordered Grandma as she put a steaming plate of shepherd's pie down on the coffee table along with a scalding cup of tea so laden with sugar I could smell it.

"Ugh, okay," I said, somehow managing to sit up.

"Drink the tea first," she ordered.

"Sure." I reached out, aghast at the puncture wounds on my palms and forearms. With shaking hands, I cupped the tea and raised it to my lips. It tasted rank, even with the sugar, and Grandma's tea always tastes delightful.

I raised an eyebrow and looked at Grandma, but she was oddly preoccupied with looking at the carpet and just said, "Drink up. All of it." So I took a slurp.

There was no burning of the throat, no spasming, or anything dramatic, just a lovely warmth that spread through my body and calmed the inner turmoil. I took several more careful sips, then drained the whole thing and somehow placed the cup back on the saucer without smashing it. Overcome, I sagged against the mound of cushions and closed my eyes for a second.

I was rudely shaken the minute I did so, and jumped. "Hey, come on, it was only for a second," I protested as Grandma moved away and sat back down.

"No, it was an hour, and we haven't got time for you to rest. Sorry, but we have to act fast if what you told us is true, and I believe it is. You can laze about later, but you're fine."

"Fine? Fine! I was crucified! I've got holes all over my body, my bones are broken, my muscles torn, my nerves fried. I was burning." A thought came to me then. "Um, hang on, when did I tell you?"

"Oh, while you were sleeping," said Grandma offhandedly, as if it were perfectly natural.

"You got into my head?" That was a strict no-no, you didn't do that, not even to your worst enemy.

"Of course not!" Grandma crossed her arms over her ample, if somewhat gravity-affected bosom, and leaned forward. "I just asked you, in a special way, and you answered. So, eat up, then we go do something heroic."

"I don't think I can even stand," I said, eyeing the food greedily.

"Don't be such a baby, you're all better now."

"Haha, you're so funny. I'm covered in…" I trailed off as I lifted an arm only to find that the wounds were little but faint red marks now. Actually realizing I was having a conversation, and wasn't just screaming, made me aware of the fact I couldn't have been in as bad a state as I'd imagined. I checked my legs, and although it hurt like a mo-fo to bend forward, it was nice to see they were all in one piece.

Sure, my thighs and calves were lumpy, not exactly the shapely curves that used to turn heads, and black and blue and purple and even orange, but they weren't smashed to smithereens and those were all bonus points in my book.

"You got a double whammy," said the Chemist as he sauntered in eating so fast half of it was spilling out of the hole in his cheek.

"You teamed up?"

"Sure did," he said happily, spitting potato everywhere.

"We had no choice," said Grandma through gritted teeth, giving the Chemist the daggers.

I could only imagine how it had gone. Two experts in their respective fields having to work together to formulate potions that would not only allow me to be taken by the Chemist, but to heal me too.

"Wow, thank you. I don't know what to say."

"Say I'll never have to do it again," said Grandma, shuddering.

"So the potions let us use your ghoul realm? And this one, it helped with my magic?"

"It was to help restore your magic, yes. And back at vampville, those were to eliminate foreign bodies and to help you pass into my realm." The Chemist looked inordinately pleased with himself, and I guess it was fair enough.

"Thank you so much. You saved my life. Both of you."

"No problem, it's what family is for, right?" said the Chemist, still so happy to be included in our family after what he'd done in the past that you wanted to say "Aah," and pat his head he was so damn excitable.

"So, you've met him, older Kane? Aren't you shocked?"

"Shocked? This is the Hidden world, Kate. I turned myself into an Elder, made babies from my skin, what's there to be shocked about? He's a good boy, and I'll take my duty as his godfather as seriously as ever."

"About that," said Kane as he came into the room. "Tell the Chemist that—"

"Simon, call me Simon," reprimanded um, Simon. Ever since he'd told me his true name he'd insisted we call him that, but everyone kept forgetting. At least Kane had an excuse.

"Fine," said Kane, in that way only a teenager in a huff can. Oh, how that made me smile. Guess some things don't change however unique an individual you are. "Please tell Simon that I can come with you. That you need me for this. I know what went on, I listened, I heard what Oskari said to you. All of it. We all know, and this means he has to be destroyed."

"You what? How? This is how you knew to come save me? What did you do?"

"He did a runner, is what he did," said Grandma. "Naughty boy."

"Kane, you could have been killed. You promised to stay here."

"I only stayed a minute, then Grandma did something wonky, some spell, and I got dragged away. Don't worry, I was only a little mouse. Nobody knew."

"Stupid boy, I was worried sick. You were gone for hours, you naughty child." Grandma smiled at him, unable to keep up her pretense of anger. It was obvious she loved him dearly and they'd bonded while I was off messing about. That was nice.

"But we saved Mother," protested Kane.

"That's not the point," argued Grandma.

It went on like that for a while but I zoned out as I performed an inner check on what was what, how I was feeling, and what damage had been inflicted.

It wasn't half as bad as I'd expected. Mainly because I'd expected to be dead.

A Plot

I ate, I showered, I even did it on my own. Sure, it hurt, but so does life, and I had that, which, for now, was enough. Grandma got a witch to collect clothes for me from home, so I dressed and hardly screamed or shouted or swore until people began banging doors closed downstairs to drown out the noise. My body was too depressing to look at, the strange lumps at every puncture point too tender to investigate with my fingers, but the bone itself had healed, just not as well as it would under normal circumstances.

Even as I dried myself the skin evened out, the swelling receded, and my flesh took on its normal lustrous, vampire sheen. My magic was rejuvenated by my joy at being alive, the lack of pin-cushionness, the food, and the potions.

Already it felt like a dream, that such things weren't possible. It was too nuts to have really happened, surely?

Nope, Oskari did this to me, did this to all of us. Plotted and planned to destroy my world, steal my son, impersonate those I loved and generally screw with me and mine.

And he'd talked of betrayal. Of me betraying him. The nerve of this guy. I'd obliterate him.

Dressed, I left Faz's old bedroom, smiling at the dated pictures on the walls and avoiding the bed pan. Grandma didn't like change so left it all as it had been for years.

"Let's go," whispered Kane as he grabbed my arm and led me slowly to the top of the stairs.

"What are you doing?" I whispered back, unsure why, but stuff like that is catching.

"We have to leave without Grandma and the Chemist. It's too dangerous for them."

I stared at my son to see if he was joking. Nope. "Dangerous? Of course it is. But you're new to all this, they have a lot, and I mean a lot, more experience than you do."

Kane shrugged his shoulders. "Maybe, but they can't do what I can. They'll cramp our style. Admit it, you were going to go alone, right?"

Damn, he was a smart kid. Not surprising, as he came from such wondrous stock. "I assume there's nothing I can say to talk you out of this? That you won't just let me leave and stay put?"

"No chance. Look what happened last time."

He had a point. With a sigh, I said, "Okay, but we need to get some things together first."

"All done. I got one of Dancer's fleet cars, loaded it up while Grandma and the Chemist were arguing in the kitchen. We're set."

"Um, you can drive? No, don't answer that. How did you get to Hidden HQ and back so fast? No, don't answer that either."

We crept down the stairs, and left.

Strange Times

The strangest, most surreal, impossible to get my head around time of my life was about to greet me. Still not really with it, I stumbled to the car, got in the passenger seat without paying due attention, and minutes later found myself being driven through the dark deserted streets of Cardiff by my son who still hadn't had his first birthday celebration. Stuff like that is enough to make a mother book herself in to the closest sanatorium, except they'd probably turn me away for being too much to handle.

I stared at my boy as he focused on the road, admired his strong jaw and smiled at the way he squinted at road signs as if seeing them for the first time, which may have been true. His driving wasn't exactly that of a seasoned professional, but he was no learner either. He drove well, just not with practiced ease, and had to concentrate rather than do it on auto-pilot. Still, the seat was soft, the new car smell was a delight, and the cool air that blew through the vents calmed my icy heart.

What was I doing? What were we doing? Should I refuse to let Kane be a part of this? It was too late for that. Oskari and his wolves would be out for my blood by now. He'd be incensed I'd escaped, furious beyond belief, and would be doing all he could to get to Kane and to find the doppels. We had to find the human shifters first, it was the only way we had a hope of resolving this monstrous screw-up and a chance of us all surviving. We needed numbers, we needed the others. We needed a bloody miracle was what we needed.

We sailed past closed stores, past off-licenses with their steel shutters down and locked, past grubby streets and gleaming buildings, racing through the night like two masked avengers out to protect the city from the bad guys.

Only problem being, I wasn't so sure we were the good guys any more.

How could we be? More to the point, how could I be?

This was my son, I should keep him safe. I told myself over and over that it was beyond that now, that unless I kept him with me at all times he was in mortal danger. But then I looked at what had happened when I was alone and at full capacity. I'd been nailed up and humiliated, left for dead. If Kane had been with me…

I'd never experienced such a turmoil of emotions before, and it took a while to understand what was happening. I was stuck with mother's anguish, unable to make a decision or think rationally and do what was best, what was most likely to see us emerge from this alive, because of my overriding concern for my son. He was safest with me, as otherwise he'd run off and do something stupid, and I knew he would have to fight and use his abilities, yet I wanted to keep him closeted and protected, wrapped up in a cocoon of love and stability that would never, could never, be his future.

We were Hidden. He was the most dangerous person in the country, and I felt like a close second.

My thoughts turned once again to Oskari and what he'd done. He betrayed me, abused my trust, my mistaken love, my need and desire for a father, and I would string him up by his pale eyes for his deceit. You know, if you could hang someone by their eyes. I'd try anyway, what did I have to lose?

On the Hunt

The city flashed by in a surreal maze of bewilderment and amazement. This Hidden life is full of unexpected twists and turns but surely there had to be limits? Kane driving me around the sleeping city mere hours after I'd been vilified and crucified by my whole community was extreme even by our standards. The fact I'd escaped and even recovered, and it was still ongoing, was nothing short of miraculous.

I made a solemn vow that day to never be a part of the vampire community in such an intimate way again. Over the years I'd had countless run-ins with either Heads or foreign visitors to our Ward, and it usually ended up with Faz killing them or half the Hidden community coming together to destroy huge numbers of our kind.

We were, when you got right down to it, no good. This had to change. Vampires had to understand that they weren't so special, that they deserved no privileged position in our world, were no better, and were often worse, than everyone else.

And the murder had to stop. The killing of innocents. For so many centuries the Council had looked the other way while the vampires killed indiscriminately, allowed them to feed from Regulars as long as it didn't cause a scene or risk us all being exposed. It was ridiculous. Human Hidden found it abhorrent and knew it was wrong. They were scared, too afraid to confront the vampires head on and deny them their feeding, fearing all out war if they did so.

But it wasn't right, and something had to be done. This extreme cruelty had spurred me into action, had opened my eyes to just how ruthless many of my kind were, and that they truly cared nothing for other people and their desire to live a happy, peaceful life. They would steal the baby from another's arms if they thought it would be to their advantage.

Not my baby. I'd fight them tooth and nail to protect him.

My life changed forever this night, my mind made up. I would no longer allow, or accept, the vampires as they were. They would change or they would perish.

"Um, Kane, where are we going? How are we supposed to find the others? Find your father?"

"Don't worry, I know where they are. We're going to get them right this minute." Kane turned and smiled at me then focused ahead as we hit a main road.

"What? We are? I don't know if I'm ready yet, strong enough."

"You are, you're stronger than you know."

"If you say so, my son. And what about you, how are you feeling? And how do you know their location?"

"I'm feeling fine now you're safe. I was very concerned. And don't worry, Mother, before this is all over we'll make sure the other vampires know what's permitted and what isn't. I'll insist."

Kane's face was set hard, a confidence in his own abilities, in what he intended to do, as if he could read my mind and come to the same conclusion. Maybe he would be all right after all, remain in touch with his human side no matter how difficult it was.

"And how do you know where they are?"

"Why, that's easy. I just followed the smell."

"I know Faz can be a bit stinky at times, but surely you can't find him in a whole city, no matter what form you take. And remember Snowdonia. You followed dwarves, not Faz."

"I remember." Kane scowled, like he should have been above such mistakes. He was going to be a competitive boy, for sure. "But no, not him. Persimmon, the shifter. I can smell a panther when I shift into her form. And that's what I did."

"Was this when you sneaked out against my express wishes?" I asked, teasing and nudging him as I smiled.

"Um, maybe. You aren't cross are you?" Kane fidgeted and glanced nervously at me.

"No, I'm just playing. I'm not cross, although in the future will you please do as I ask? I know you're special, but sometimes a mother knows best."

Kane nodded. It was easy to forget that he was still an immature child, and I had to keep that in mind and treat him accordingly. He may be powerful beyond compare but he was a boy nonetheless, and a teenage one at that. Probably the worst combination possible.

"So, where are we going?"

"Somewhere unexpected." Kane turned and gave me a smile that looked so like Faz that I burst out crying.

And he was right, it sure was unexpected.

To the Rescue

Kane parked up in the city center at one of the multi-story car parks. He turned the engine off and we sat there not saying a word, just listening to the ticking of the engine as it cooled quickly. It was deserted, no signs of life, just a few random cars belonging to those working night shifts with nowhere else to park. Probably people stocking shelves in the stores, or maybe it was the insomniacs, or those who frequented the secretive clubs that remained open all night for the dedicated drinkers. Or even Hidden who only found peace and the chance to be who they really were when night descended.

We got out after several minutes, and I found it a struggle. Sitting down had not been a good idea. I was so stiff, and everything hurt so much, I couldn't imagine facing a horde of doppels and having any chance of dealing with them. But then I remembered who I was, what I was, and what I was fighting for. Magic came to my rescue, as it always did.

Ink activated, just a tingle under leather trousers, white shirt, and long leather jacket, clothes Grandma had obviously felt I'd need for what was to come. Energy coursed through my veins and the hurt went away. I stretched for a few minutes while Kane rummaged about in the car, shook out the stiffness of newly formed muscle, let joints and bones as fresh as a newborn's feel weight and integrate properly.

My body was a single, finely tuned machine now, as if a switch had been flipped because of the extremes of my torture. I could feel no difference between flesh and the unknowable Empty, or the wonders of the ink for that matter. It was a closed system, functioning as one, and the power was heightened, magnified, and stronger than ever.

I could only think of it as a kick-start to make it work in unison, a symbiosis of something born of the natural world and the imposed magic of the vampire nature. It was one; I was fine. I was dangerous.

This realization brought home how incredibly powerful Kane must have been. I felt alive and brimming with energy now I'd accepted this was my true self, how must he feel? He could do anything, be anything, and it wasn't disparate parts of his make-up combining, it was simply who he was. He'd become vampire and that merely became another part of him.

The bloody icing on a very volatile cake.

Kinda scary if you think about it, and if you weren't his mother.

But I was, and we were dangerous. We'd get them back, we'd deal with this, and we'd do it together.

"Let's go," said Kane. "Come on, no time to lose."

I trusted him, so I followed him out of the car park.

A Surprise

"Look, I know you're young, and I know you're excited about, er, being a teenager, but you aren't old enough to drink." I felt kind of foolish for even saying it, but it was true. He may be an uber vampire-wizard, shifter, and who knew what else, but he was under age and that was that.

"Haha. We aren't here so I can try my first pint, we're here because this is where they are." Kane stared at the door with such ferocity I was surprised it didn't melt.

"You muppet. They won't be in here. You must have got your scents mixed up, or picked up on an old one. How could they possibly be here?"

"What better place to hide than in plain sight? Okay, it's not out in the open, but it's perfect if you are capable of what they are. Mother, I've trailed them all over the city and they've moved around a lot, hiding in different places, but this is where they are now, where they've been for some time. They're inside."

I looked at the door dubiously, unconvinced. Why would they hide out here? How could they hide out here? Duh, because they were doppels, of course. But my friends and family weren't, and everyone recognized them. But nobody else knew they were missing, did they? I tried to think about everything that had happened, and realized that hardly anyone knew they'd been taken as it would cause way too much turmoil and, frankly, utter carnage if people knew. So it would be business as usual. If, and it was a big if, none of them warned anyone else about what was happening.

Guess there was only one way to find out.

I tore off the sign that said closed, something Brewster Bunker, troll owner and always mindful of the capacity of the place, often stuck to the door to deter anyone but Hidden. Then I pressed my hand to the battered steel in a special way known to all Hidden customers, and another way to stop Regulars when things got heated inside, and pushed open the door.

"Just don't nick any drinks," I warned Kane.

"I won't." He smiled as we entered the Hidden Club.

As You Were

The stench of Hidden hit like a smack in the face with a goblin's sweaty sock filled with Gorgonzola. The thick cloud from myriad smoking devices that many Hidden had permanently attached to their lips—Brewster wasn't bothered by the smoking ban—made vision from the top of the stairs to this basement den of iniquity hazy, and it made us both cough until magic stirred to scrub our lungs.

As usual, the noise was close to deafening, loud conversations, arguments, and name-calling the usual cacophony.

We descended slowly, and I made sure Kane stayed behind me. My enhanced eyesight studied the drunken revelers, the solitary drinkers slumped over the small tables, or the groups of various races bashing each other with the red lamps Brewster put out each night like clockwork, only to have to replace the next day.

As we shuffled across the floor, trying to avoid getting stuck by the lake of spilled alcohol, I recognized many familiar faces. Some smiled, several nodded, plenty scowled. I still wasn't the most popular person in Hidden parts, especially amongst wizards. It may have had something to do with me being partly responsible for hundreds dying at the hands of ghouls, but I'd been miffed and they were rude.

So, business as usual by the looks of it. No sign of Faz or the others though, just Hidden doing what they did best here. Drink, fight, argue, throw magic of a limited variety around—Brewster would break your head if you did too much damage.

We stopped at the bar and both leaned against the polished wooden counter and checked out the clientele properly. Everything seemed normal because it was so mad. Dwarves played Guess the Hammer, a strange game that involved them whacking each other across the cheek and the other guessing the weight of the mighty hammer used to smack them off their chairs.

Goblins hunched over tables, moodily looking for the slightest reason to start a fight, wizards sat in small groups, many of them pissed and constantly having to drag their straggly beards out of strong, thick lager, and several other Hidden species did what came naturally. Meaning they were hitting each other or hurling insults about their mothers.

I tugged at Kane's arm and we turned to face the bar. Brewster was at the far end, immobile, but I waved and caught his eye. He ambled over, then asked, "Wot you want?"

"Two lemonades please, Brewster." I gave him my most winning smile but he just grunted then poured the drinks.

He placed them down in front of us on two beer mats, then held out a hand for payment. I frowned but paid him, nonetheless. Maybe he'd started a new policy of requiring cash straight away rather than paying up at the end of the night or whenever you felt like it.

Then he said, "Boy not old enough. Against law."

"He's older than he looks," I said, smiling at Kane.

Brewster grunted then shuffled off to stand at the far end and look menacing.

"That was odd," I said, staring after him.

"What was?"

"He doesn't usually care about anyone's age. Not Hidden anyway."

Kane gave me a funny look, and waited. I shook my head; I didn't know what he was trying to say.

After it began to get weird I said, "Okay, spill it, mister. What's up?"

"It was odd because he's a doppel. They all are. At least, most of them. Not all. I told you, hiding in plain sight."

"But there must be, what, sixty, seventy Hidden in here. You can't be serious?" I scanned the room but everything seemed exactly how you'd expect.

Kane raised an eyebrow, like I was being a little slow. Guess I was, but I had an excuse. Crucifixion, remember?

"Um, okay, so they've cloned Brewster. And not very well." The more I watched him, the odder he was acting. He was almost smiling, and he somehow looked smug. And he kept glancing our way, something Brewster would never do. He had being an ignorant bartender down to a fine art.

"They've done it in a hurry, so they can hide out. I bet at least half the Hidden here are doppels. It's why there aren't any imps."

"Or other creatures that can just appear and disappear. They can't do that, can they?"

"No."

"Ah, so we know we can trust imps. At least, as far as you ever can." I wondered where Intus was, what she was up to. I hadn't seen her in a while, none of us had. Not since the first few days after Kane was born, when she came and insisted on giving him a lava bath that almost got very messy and very scalding, only being dissuaded by being offered unlimited Marmite if she promised to refrain from burning a newborn to death with molten rock.

"And there are quite a few true Hidden, not impostors," said Kane. "Probably the ones fighting."

"Yeah, probably." I studied the crowd with deeper focus, trying to figure out who was who, but it wasn't easy.

Hidden act odd at the best of times, and give them potent alcohol and it can get seriously freaky, very fast.

A wizard wandered by on the way to the bathroom but halted and turned back a moment after passing us. He swayed on the spot and tried to focus, then leaned forward until I could smell his breath. I thought he was going to fall over.

"You did the… did the right thing," he said, slurring his words. "The… the ones that attacked you, they were wrong."

"Um, thanks. That's very nice of you to say so." And it was. Friendly wizards hadn't been queuing up to say nice things of late.

"Welcome." With that, he belched loudly, teetered backwards, managed to stay upright, and weaved his way to the bathroom.

"That was nice of him," said Kane.

"It was." It made me pleased to know not everyone hated me just because I could use magic like they could.

Then someone threw a lamp at my head.

Furtive Glances

I ducked, smiling despite the seriousness of the situation. Some things never change, and there were definitely plenty of true Hidden here, not doppel impostors.

I scanned the faces again, and as the minutes ticked by it became obvious who was who. Most customers either ignored me or scowled, maybe smiled, but some kept glancing our way when they thought I wasn't looking. They were the doppels, unable to remain in character because they didn't know what I was up to or what had happened since Kane had been taken away to be changed into the One. Sure, they would have had reports that something had gone down, but they wouldn't know what. Would only be able to go by what they'd found at the site. And that was a lot of blood and plenty of corpses.

They were running scared. Unable to leave as they knew the One was still alive, but unsure what to do. Guess they'd have people out looking for us, same as

Oskari would. As the night wore on, the doppels began to take more of an interest in Kane, putting two and two together. I knew this was a bad idea, bringing him with me. Now they knew we were here, and what he looked like.

Hidden stirred, moved into groups that gave them away as certain races don't enjoy a chat or a friendly pint together, especially not when some are goblins. They were panicking, trying to come up with the best plan.

Where was Faz?

I turned to Kane and asked. "Are they here?"

"Yes, but I don't know where. Not unless I shift and track them."

"No, don't do that. Not now. We don't want everyone knowing what you can do. Especially not the doppels. Let's leave it like that."

Kane shrugged. "If you're sure?"

I nodded. "I am."

We leaned back, acting extra casual, but I could almost see the magic extending from our bodies, slender tendrils of power that expanded our auras. Everyone gave us a wide berth without actually seeing this magical menace, but their bodies made them change direction, even the pissed ones.

The room took on a definite edge and the glances were no longer merely furtive. We were now being stared at with downright hostility. Those who weren't doppels must have sensed something, and over the next fifteen minutes or so the place was half emptied as

Hidden suddenly decided they'd had enough and should call it a night.

As the door slammed shut on the last of them, the room took on an instant frosty vibe. There was something else though. They were in awe, maybe of me and Kane, as after all, I was the mother of the One. But violence bubbled beneath the surface, and they would have him no matter the cost to me. This was their prophet and they wanted him to lead them, be one of them, but more than anything else they wanted to control him.

Bodies shifted. One stood, then others followed suit. Soon they were all standing, closing in on us.

I waved a finger languidly, and said, "Tut, tut, I wouldn't do that if I were you. We just want those you took, nothing more. Give them to us and nobody has to get hurt."

A man approached, just a normal looking guy. Long straight hair, stubble, jeans, and a check shirt. "He is the One. He has been chosen. He will help us become what we were destined to be."

"No, he bloody well won't," I said. "Kane hasn't even started school yet. He can't go off gallivanting. It's past his bedtime too."

"Mother!"

"Just messing with these guys. But I am right."

"He's the One." The guy said it with awe, and there were gasps from the others as the truth was confirmed.

"No, he's my son. Your kind changed him, made him something he shouldn't be yet. That's on you, and that's as far as this goes. You tortured me, you put his life in peril. Well, you saw what happened to those in the wilds, you saw what I did. You want more of the same?"

"The One will be ours. He will allow us to rule."

Kane stepped forward, perfectly calm. "I won't, you know. You hurt Mother, you almost killed me. You will pay. I owe you nothing. You are misguided and have chosen the wrong path."

He was damn impressive because he spoke with such utter authority, his body language that of somebody who felt no threat, was at ease in this situation. I was glad I was on his side. He was scary, intimidating.

"But the prophesy. You are to help us succeed. You had to be changed, forced to grow up, and then you would lead us, show us the way. Tell us how to rule."

I shook my head at the sheer mindless acceptance these people had for a prophecy probably handed down for thousands of years and warped who knew how many times. Why did they believe this? Why had this myth continued for so long? And why the hell were we standing around chatting to these numpties?

"Enough!" I warned. "Where is the Head? Where is the shifter? The young wizard? Where's my fucking husband?"

"Mother!"

"Oh, sorry. Where is my fudging husband?" I turned to Kane. "That better?"

"Yes, much."

I nodded.
Things kicked off.

Death Raineth

The spokesman took another step forward, his intentions clear. His features morphed, mimicking me, and then the others flickered, their heads and bodies vibrating too fast to see. We were faced with a roomful of clones, split pretty evenly between Kane and me.

They'd tried this trick on me before, and although it was freaky and disorientating, I wasn't about to let it mess with my head.

I willed the magic up from the depths, felt my eyes snap to black and my teeth snick down. Ink activated, engorged with clear, wholesome energy I would corrupt and use to wreak havoc. Kane drifted close and I saw him do likewise, his eyes so black they terrified me, his teeth so long and sharp and already dripping the vampire's tear. I wanted to weep for his loss of innocence.

Nonetheless, we lifted our arms in unison and mother and son blasted the hell out of the guy in front. Blasted the hell out of a perfect copy of me. As his head exploded, I gulped. A psychoanalyst would have a field day with this. We'd just killed me. That can't be good for your kid's mental wellbeing.

"Change back, right now," I ordered, but nobody had eyes for me, nobody was listening.

Kane stepped forward, looking menacing and handsome, regal and as though he was born to have others bow at his feet. And that's exactly what the doppels were doing. They all switched back to their regular form, or what I assumed were, and every single one of them, barring the guy with the exploded head, bent to kneel.

"Lead us, rule us, teach us. Show us the way." This time it was a woman who spoke, and she was beautiful. In fact she was stunning. Long black hair curled down across her shoulders, cupping her elven face like a lover's hands. Her eyes were dark pits of desire, and she licked her swollen lips as she breathed deep, almost panting as she stared at Kane.

This couldn't be good, certainly wasn't right, and my motherly instincts kicked in. Kane was way, and I mean way, too young for any of that nonsense. Yes, he was too immature to be dealing out death too, but I wasn't about to give the go-ahead for any naked fun times, however screwed up that made me.

Able to see him with detachment because we weren't being attacked full-scale like last time, I looked at him maybe the way the doppels saw him. This group, the last of them in the city I assumed, were the ones not directly involved in the kidnap, were clearly tasked with keeping Faz and the others so they could copy them, so they'd had time to consider what had happened, probably come up with all kinds of crazy reasons why their kind had been slaughtered.

It was clear that they idolized Kane, and I guess to some degree me too because I was his mother. It probably wouldn't stop them killing me if I got in their way, but this was what they'd waited so long for and now here he was, the man himself. Boy, he was a boy, I reminded myself.

Kane seemed taller, his features more defined, the inner strength shining through as magic simmered beneath the surface, imbuing him with a radiance that made him almost angelic, although he was more an angel of death than of peace. His presence dominated the room, and he really did look like a leader of men. Someone to look up to, seek guidance from. A king.

"What do you want from me?" he asked.

"We want you to help us. Let us become the true rulers of the Hidden. Guide us, show us the way. Let us emerge from the shadows. We are few, this is all of us left now. We place our lives in your hands." There were nods of agreement, murmurs of worship, pleas to be taken under his wing, and I understood that this was more complicated than I'd expected.

Kane turned to me, just as confused as I was, and asked, "Mother?"

I shrugged my shoulders; this wasn't what I'd expected. What I had expected was to break bones and bash heads until we found everyone and then let Dancer do as he saw fit to those who'd wronged us.

Maybe it was best to stick to the plan. It was that or just kill them all now, and no way could I let Kane be involved in the massacre of those not actually attacking us. They had acted terribly, kidnapped my son, forced him to change, but that wasn't this group. These were the ones waiting to be led, not those who had headed up the change imposed on Kane. Did they even know what had happened?

"Hand over the others and we'll see what we can do," I said, casting an inquiring glance at Kane.

"Yes, return Father and his friends and we can talk. I will not deal with you knowing you have them. Are they all alive?"

"They are. They are, ah, not cooperating, so making perfect copies has been hard. So you found out? You know we have them?"

"Are you all stupid?" I blurted. "Of course we bloody know! Why do you think we're here? You lot kidnapped them, stole my son, turned him into a boy before his time, of course we bloody know." What was with these people? Weren't they listening? Too focused on Kane, I guess.

"We were unsure what you had been told, what you had found out," said the woman, still on her knees, still drooling over Kane. "We found the bodies, but little else. We thought maybe they had sinned and the One punished them. But we waited, went ahead with our plans, waited for you."

"Hell, what is wrong with you people? Look, where are the others? Tell us then we'll see about the rest. But if you don't start talking I'll kill every last one of you."

The woman stood, and I swear she wiggled her hips as she sashayed back to the others then cast a sexy glance over her shoulder. I watched Kane but he seemed completely unfazed, didn't react in the slightest.

They spoke quietly for a moment then she turned and said, "We will give them to you. We just wanted to make the future perfect for the One. You would never have known it wasn't your father, we promise."

"Yet you would have killed my mother." It wasn't a question, it was a statement of fact. "And you would have killed my father, impersonated him. Tricked me." Kane's anger was rising so I hastily put a hand to his shoulder to calm him.

"Later, okay? For now let's just get them back. These people are obsessed, and the obsessed, the indoctrinated, they do crazy things."

"You can find them—"

The door smashed open, and I mean smashed into tiny pieces, and Oskari's aide stood at the top of the stairs. He surveyed the scene below with cold detachment, then walked slowly down, followed by vampire after vampire.

Nobody moved, nobody said a word.

More and more vampires filed down, and they kept on coming, backing up the stairs.

"Kill them all, apart from the boy," snarled the aide.

A Bit Crowded

Brewster Bunker, wherever he was, would not be happy about this. He put up with a certain amount of damage as part of running his business, but strictly forbade full out war in his club for obvious reasons. Like he didn't want the building destroyed for starters.

The doppels moved forward and I readied to blast any that got too close, but then as they formed a barrier in front of us and turned to face the vampires I understood they weren't trying to do anything apart from protect us.

I should have told them it was a lost cause, that they didn't stand a chance, but that's not the kind of pep talk you want before you go into battle.

Actually, they kind of surprised me with their ferocity and refusal to be intimidated. The vampires amassed at one end of the room, the doppels and us at the other, just the tables between us.

Then they did something smart. They each morphed into a perfect replica of the aide, damn Sigma, and then rushed forward before anyone had a chance to react. They grouped close around him and then the fighting started.

Sigma was a blur of vampire ferocity as he bit and slashed and snapped bone, more than a match for what were basically Hidden with no special magical abilities. They rallied and they fought back, attacking him in force to overpower him, but it was futile at best, a suicide mission. The vampires didn't know who to attack at first, but once they zoned in on the only Sigma able to move fast and who was the center of attention, they sprang into action.

"If they kill all the doppels we won't get to find out where Faz is," I shouted to Kane. "He clearly isn't here."

"And the vampires need to be punished," said Kane, nodding in agreement.

He was right, of course, same as I was. The vampires wanted Kane just as much as the doppels, more so, and were in a much better position to make it happen. Oskari was hell-bent on having Kane, was scared of my son and what lay ahead if he wasn't under his care, and had the power to obtain him.

Unless we taught him a lesson he'd never forget.

I don't know which of us moved first, maybe we did it together, but next thing I knew mother and son were attacking the vampires, our own kind, with a wild ferocity born of anger, maybe even hatred for what they'd done to me, what they wished to do to Kane, and for their very nature. That we were like them, but a thing apart, made the emotions more intense, for we refused to become as they were, yet did unspeakable acts to protect ourselves from becoming as cold and uncaring.

Boy, this world is messed up, and so full of contradictions, but we killed to save ourselves, to retain our humanity, and that's one tough set of statements to get your head around.

We didn't fight to protect the doppels because of any kindness, we did it to get answers and to find those we cared about. These were dangerous individuals, probably the most dangerous there were, and I was well aware how much trouble even a single doppel could cause to our world if they impersonated someone important, and they obviously had no compunction about doing exactly that, yet we had to protect at least one.

The ruse to impersonate Sigma had failed, so they reverted back to their own features.

Kane and I joined the fray in earnest, Kane focusing on protecting me while I went to town on the vampires. Most were easy to eliminate, the vampire confidence and belief they were superior to everyone else playing against them as it always did. They were so full of their own bullshit it always came as a total surprise when they looked down to discover their heart had been ripped out or a limb or two had been yanked off.

I became death incarnate. My ink swirled and engorged my system with magic and my hands let forth mighty blasts of destruction that chewed holes through flesh and obliterated heads, melted skin, and crumbled bone. There was no stopping me once I was in the zone, almost a flow state where each movement was precise, no energy wasted, nothing on my mind. I acted on instinct, knowing Kane had my back and was more than capable of looking after mummy.

The bodies piled up, the number of doppels outnumbering the vampires. Several doppels were practitioners and they blasted as best they could but it was clear they were no adepts, that whoever had made the veil back where all this began and Kane turned were not part of this group. Vampires dodged magic and appeared next to the users, clamping down hard and deadly on their necks and gaining power as they destroyed the doppels for their treachery, for not handing over Kane when they had the chance. For betraying Oskarl.

I managed to get close to Sigma and without taking the time to let him see who was ending his life, I gripped his head in my hands as he bit down on the neck of a doppel and I squeezed, shunted all my strength into my hands. The ink on my forearms strained against my jacket as terrible forces boosted flesh and bone. His head popped, brains and splinters of bone erupting in all directions.

Someone screamed behind me. I whirled in time to witness Kane punch out at a charging vampire. The guy just kept on coming until Kane's arm was straight through his rib cage. Kane pushed him off with a foot then scanned for trouble.

"Grab the girl. Let's get out of here," I shouted to him.

He nodded and darted to the seductress. He threw her over his shoulder and sped to my side. I surged forward, cleared a path to the stairs, which was easy as nearly everyone was dead, and took them three at a time, Kane right behind me.

The cool air hit, fortifying me. More vampires were coming down the street, and I knew there would be scores, maybe hundreds more on the way. The word was out.

Wasting no time, we sped through the night, away from this place, from the death. From my husband.

Doing a Solid

We found ourselves at the castle in the heart of the city, not far from the Millennium Stadium, across the road from the museum and opposite some great pubs. Everything was closed, locked up until morning, but when you're being chased by vampire hordes, people think your son is the chosen one, and you have no way of knowing who, if anyone, you can trust, then a fortified castle with high walls, open spaces, and plenty of vantage points, plus no people, is quite a good idea.

I made short work of the lock and slammed the massive wood and iron door shut after we entered, did a little boosting of the entry to stop it being easily destroyed, then we hightailed it into the grounds.

Dotted around the grassed interior, protected by crumbling walls, were random stones and low walls, markers for rooms long ago fallen. Shapes large and small loomed out of the darkness, but one in particular seemed more menacing than the others.

In a panic, and not wanting any more surprises, I sprinted toward it, leaving the others by the front walls, and skidded to a halt, mistimed, so slammed into a very large, very human-shaped lump of rock.

"Brewster?" I asked, stepping back and looking up at the owner of the Hidden Club. The troll remained motionless, stood immobile as I waved my hand in front of his eyes. He was like a statue, one the artist had given up on halfway through, deciding the rough, uneven look would soon be in vogue.

Kane appeared at my side, his hand gripping the woman's bare upper arm tightly but not in a cruel way, just enough to ensure she couldn't yank free. "What's wrong with him? Why is he here?"

"No idea." Trolls were slow, but this was ridiculous. Why had the doppels put him here? Or had they?

"He escaped, crushed several of us and simply wandered off," said the woman.

I turned to her. "How long ago?"

"Many hours."

This was worrying, worrying in a way I didn't understand, just knew was bad. But we didn't have time to hang around to figure it out. The doppels, the few who still survived, had Faz somewhere, meaning that soon the vampires would find him. There was no good end to this, not unless we did something, and fast.

"We have to go back." I could see no other way. "I'm sorry, but I can't think of anything else to do." I grabbed the woman's beautiful face, her lush hair tangling around my fingers, and turned her eyes from Kane to me. "Where were they? Were they really in the club?"

She nodded.

"Where?" I hissed, my frustration and sense of impending doom crushing the air out of me until I felt like screaming and hitting something really, really hard.

"Mother!" warned Kane, a sense of panic in his voice.

I turned from Kane back to the woman, only to find I was squeezing her so tight she was turning blue. Her skin writhed beneath my fingers, malleable like semi-molten plastic, reconfiguring into face after face. Flashing by many times a second as if trying to find a configuration that would ease the pressure.

I loosened my grip but I didn't let go, and she returned to her beautiful features. She gasped for air, opened her mouth a little, straining against my grip, and said, "I won't run, my people are all dead now. I will follow the One, and the Mother. Be yours. You have no reason to fear me."

Staring into her deep, dark eyes, I sensed the truth of it, that she was awed and besotted by my son, that she believed there were none of her own kind left. That they were dead and she had somehow managed to position herself to be of use to the person she believed was her true leader. "Ugh, with eyes like yours, plus the body, you're always going to be dangerous."

My hand dropped loose to my side and I tried to relax my tense shoulders but I was wound tighter than a dwarf's braid. "Fine, but you run you die. Understood?"

The woman nodded. "Beaut, I'm Beaut."

"Of course you are," I sighed, stress levels rising as she stared at Kane with adoration tinged with lust. I noted Kane's very adult reaction as his neck flushed and his pupils dilated. Great, this was all I needed. A randy teenager on top of everything else going on.

"Beaut," whispered Kane, and I swear he smiled at this woman, this person who would have seen me dead and him locked in an enforced role as imprisoned leader-cum-mascot for a bunch of deranged doppels. Guess that's kids and hormones for you, makes them stupid no matter how smart they are.

"Where are they?" I asked again, so close to ripping her throat out I had to grab my own arm to stop it finding blood like a heat-seeking missile.

"We had them under the stage, the platform at the end of the room. The club is not what it seems. It's a most unusual place."

I pictured it in my mind, the small stage where the Chemist performed his stand-up and other acts risked life and limb out of an extreme masochistic desire to be ridiculed by powerful, drunk magical beings. There was no way they could be there, there wasn't room.

"You're lying to me," I growled, ready to rip her head clean off now.

"She's not," said Kane, as I shifted forward.

"I swear it's the truth. There's a whole other world underneath. One of us had heard of it, a tale from decades ago, and it was true. A warren of rooms beneath the club, used to hide in."

Guess it did make sense. After all, the trapdoor in the dressing room hid a series of tunnels and catacombs that led directly to the cemetery. This was probably part of that underground system but had been separated at some point.

"Let's go," I ordered, giving Brewster one more glance.

We began to walk off but I turned at the sound of rock grinding on rock.

Brewster was striding toward us and he didn't look happy. In fact, he looked exceedingly angry. Before I could say a word, he grabbed Beaut's head in his hand and squeezed. Bone and brain squirted between his fingers as he released her and she slumped to the grass.

He turned to us, raised a hand, and I swear his usually dead looking eyes glowed with an inner fire more freaky than any Hidden's I'd seen before.

Like the night wasn't bad enough already.

Ending

I stepped in front of Kane and readied myself, but Brewster lowered his arm and his deep, rumbling voice like a mountain with vocal chords said, "Woman barred."

The fire died in his eyes, back to his usual stoic self, but I swear I caught a flicker of a lip twitch. Was he making a joke?

"She was helping us." Kane moved to my side, stared at the body, and tensed.

What kind of world was this where my son was witness to grotesquery after grotesquery? This was so messed up I didn't even know where to begin. What kind of person was I when such a sight became the norm, didn't turn my stomach and make me puke? It's easy to talk about this stuff but it doesn't give the visceral, true sense of how gruesome it is to witness such things. I'm so far gone there's no hope for me. This wasn't right, none of it was. Squashed heads and death after death; utter madness.

I calmed Kane with a look and the anger subsided. He understood, not only that Brewster had to have his revenge, but that the troll had been right, justified in his course of action.

"What happened to you?" I asked.

"Doppels took over bar. Brewster knew had to leave, that time has come."

"Time? Time for what?"

As this immortal creature of the very earth itself opened his mouth to speak, my phone rang, right on cue. I fished it out and wasn't surprised to see that it was Oskari, his personal number calling. What an honor. Not.

"Don't tell me, you have them and you want to trade?"

"How very astute of you, Kate. Do we have a deal?"

"Of course we don't have a deal. Are you out of your sick mind? I guess you killed all the doppels, got your revenge, but do you think Faz or the others would want you to have Kane? No, I love them all, and this breaks my heart, which I have, unlike you, but the answer is no. No deal."

"You disappoint me, Kate. Very well, so be it. There is plenty of time for Kane to come to me. But your husband, your friends, the wizard child, the Head, they will pay in your stead for your treachery."

"Oskari, let me tell you something right now, and you better listen good. Whatever you do, whether they survive or not, I'm going to kill you. I'm going to kill you and take everything away from you. You hear me?"

"Many have tried, my dear. Yet I'm still here. You betrayed your own kind, you're a disgrace to your House. My House."

"Maybe it's time to clean house," I said softly, but he'd already hung up.

Back Again

"Mother, what did he say?" asked Kane.

"Wait, I'm trying to think." Brewster seemed happy enough to stand immobile and let me have a moment, but Kane was antsy so I told him the truth, although he'd heard my side of the conversation so there wasn't much left to say. "Now, let me think."

The problem with many magic users is that they rely on their magic, same as all Hidden rely on their nature to lead their actions, rather than taking the time to think things through and use their wits. I may not be the smartest, but I'm no dummy either, and I knew Oskari certainly wasn't. I pushed the fear over Faz down and away, looked at this as an outsider, trying to think things through logically to consider my next move without emotion.

Oskari knew we'd come for our friends and family, knew others would be incensed by what had happened and that now he risked outright war and an attack on his fortified home. The vampires had been attacked many times over the years, Faz even led an assault that saw a massive shift in the dynamic of vampire politics, and the last thing he'd do was sit there and wait for every wizard and enemy in the city, then the country, to come deal with him for what he'd done.

I convinced myself that he'd be on the move, taking the vampires with him until this got resolved. This was crunch time, no turning back now his plans were revealed. Maybe he thought I'd keep quiet, maybe he thought I'd hand Kane over, or maybe he had his own plans and was one step ahead of me. He was smart, had hundreds of years more experience than me, and knew his actions were way more than Hidden would stand for.

No, he'd leave, maybe keep his captives alive in case he could use them, but he would not sit still and wait for the backlash. He would seek power, a way to put the odds further in his favor, and above all else he would be putting into action a way to get Kane.

Then I understood, and I turned to Brewster, knowing even before I asked that my hunch was right, that this was bigger than I'd imagined and a lot more scary.

"You were connecting with the hivemind, right? You were connecting to the other trolls."

"We became one. We share. Know everything."

Hell, this was like an epic conversation by troll standards. I knew the truth about trolls, about the shared experience between each and every one of them since their awakening. They are sentinels, recording all of human history, and it makes you appreciate them in a whole new light. But why now? I knew, was afraid to ask, but did anyway.

"Because of Kane?"

Brewster nodded. "But not just boy, because of you."

"Me? What about me?"

"Not time. Must go."

"Let me guess, back to Snowdonia, right?" This was all coming together now, the pieces slotting into place. Why the doppels had maneuvered us into going there in the first place, how they'd turned Kane into what he now was. Why there were so many damn Hidden in those parts.

"Magic strong. Worlds collide. The lines flow." With that, Brewster stomped over the body of Beaut, heedless of such an act, squishing her flat. Guts and worse spurted from tears in flesh made by the pressure of tons of rock. He didn't stop at the magic-infused entrance, just smashed right through, picking up speed as he went until by the time he hit he was moving so fast it would make a vampire jealous.

"Bloody hell, he's full of surprises." I was astonished. Trolls didn't move fast, they were often slower than the glaciers many emerged from.

"This is serious, isn't it?" asked Kane.

"Kind of," I replied, distracted. What did he mean, this was about me too? I was nothing special, not really. But I'd known, somehow felt that everything leading back to Snowdonia. I just wasn't sure why.

There may have been strong magical forces converging there, making all this madness a reality, but Cardiff was a powerful place too, center of numerous ley lines.

At least I knew where Oskari was headed. Maybe we could intercept him and save the others before it was too late. But a part of me was already saying goodbye to my husband and friends, because, when it came down to it, I know vampires, and they are fucking evil.

Disobedient Children

"We should go tell Grandma, and the Chemist, see if they have a way to help us out," I said, feeling ragged like life was chipping away at my body. Pains returned, aches deep in my bones. A terrifying sadness threatened to consume me, to make me ineffective and nowhere near up to the task that lay ahead.

As the work done by the potions of earlier waned, I relived every damn nail. My nerves flared and I winced and gasped as I doubled over, but I didn't let it win. I allowed it to pass over and leave me capable but running dangerously low on energy and sheer willpower. I would not succumb. I couldn't. So I stood, turned to my son, but he wasn't there.

"I have to save Father. I'll give myself to them," shouted Kane from the shattered gate before he disappeared.

"No, you can't!" Not caring how exhausted I was, I ran after him, turned at the gate, but he was gone.

I was alone in Cardiff.

A Mother's Fury

Something snapped inside and something dark emerged. I knew I couldn't outrun Kane, that he was more powerful and probably more dangerous than me. I also knew he was smart and would take a route I couldn't follow. Don't ask me why, guess it was because it was exactly what I would have done in his place.

He would get to Oskari before me, and every damn vampire in the city would then converge on them to ready for the trouble Oskari knew was coming his way.

Time to even out the odds. Do something unexpected.

Death came to Cardiff this night, death on an epic scale doled out by a single woman who would do anything to save her child.

It had been a long time coming at any rate. If the Council refused to take care of business in the way they should have long ago, then I'd damn well do it for them.

I was, still am for my sins, vampire. I knew them all in my city, knew where they lived, knew their past, knew their good and their many bad points. Knew who abided by our rules, who killed only those who deserved to die, and who killed for pleasure and hurt their victims for the perverse fun of it.

I paid the bad guys, and trust me, there were plenty, a visit. First the Hidden Club, where some remained, most already leaving and heading down the street, called by the communal consciousness of the vampires.

The calling to follow Oskari became stronger by the minute as he moved away from the city as I'd expected. They all paid for the nails they'd thrust into my flesh, for the joy they took in such an act. Magic came from somewhere dark and bottomless, and they were mowed down before most knew what was happening. I tore and ripped and broke necks and smashed faces to pulp in a frenzy that did not abate until the city center was cleaned.

I didn't even get to use the gun, as it was back at Oskari's, stripped from me along with so much else. It would have been nice to have the backup, but what's a poor vampire gal to do?

Several trolls seemed to trail my every move, somehow appearing once punishment was meted out. They acted as cleanup crew as I killed in dark alleys and places no cameras outside of our control could see.

I returned to Vampire HQ, the place manned by a skeleton crew that soon became less than skeletal once I finished with them.

Power seemed to grow as my violence escalated until it was utterly out of control, and within an hour I had destroyed every single remaining mean, nasty vampire that deserved nothing less. But most had left, chasing after Oskari or already moving with him into the wilderness where he seemed to believe he could fight and win against other Hidden.

Or maybe he knew Kane and I would discover where he was going, and it was done on purpose. A ruse.

I gave up thinking and just acted. Decided not to involve Grandma, the Chemist, or even Delilah, to keep them out of it because I loved them and couldn't stand to see anyone else I cared about put in danger.

Finally I was finished, the trolls always present, cleaning up, stomping to mush, or dragging away those I had put an end to. Magic gnawed at my insides, craving more release. My ink was fat and backed up with thick power, my body thrummed and vibrated and dangerous sparks shot from my flesh as I became something pure, something born of violence.

An Angel of Death.

Breaking the Law

I returned to the car, sane and aware enough to know I couldn't run all the way to Snowdonia. I grabbed the key from the wheel arch where Kane had left it—he's so smart—got in, covering the seats in blood and unmentionable bits of dead vampire, and then fished in my bag and rifled through the data sticks.

Hyped, but crashing hard, I turned the engine on, cranked up the air conditioning until my teeth chattered, and sped into the night listening to Napalm Death. Next came Extreme Noise Terror, then Suicidal Tendencies, which maybe wasn't the best of ideas, then Bon Jovi for light relief. But it set my nerves jangling, made me more antsy than listening to jazz, so back to Carcass, then Corrosion of Conformity, and all the while I grew increasingly manic, stress levels unmaintainable. Every drumbeat, every scream, every guitar riff telling me my family, my son, my husband, was dead, being tortured, or worse.

Oh, the things I imagined, the hatred I felt for my own kind, for vampire, and I can't tell you how many times I caught sight of one running through the night and I screeched to a halt, tracked them down and did terrible things. I also mowed down a few who remained in the road, defying me, opening the car door to check they were dead while the music blared and the night turned red with blood on the asphalt and death in my heart.

Every second took me closer, and every minute made it less likely I would save anyone. I was bursting with tension, my muscles knotted and practically detaching from my body they were stretched so taut.

The car suddenly filled with a thick, pungent smoke, the stink of sulfur, a rotten egg stench that clawed at my throat so bad I swerved, blinded by the effects. I slammed on the brakes on a thankfully empty road.

"Hello, Mrs. Kate, got any—"

"Not now, Intus," I snapped, as I wound the window down so I could see enough to pull over into a passing spot.

Intus' ears flattened against the side of her head and her forked tail drooped and thudded against the dashboard. I say thud, more like a quiet tap, but that's because she's an imp that can easily fit in the palm of your hand. "Um, sorry." Intus slapped a hand over her mouth in shock—imps don't apologize often, they do stuff that drives you nuts as it's their role in life and about as much a part of them as their red hides.

"No, it's me. Things are a little stressful. Er, very stressful. Okay, I'm driving myself insane and I think I'm about to lose my mind if I haven't already.

"The bit of bother in Cardiff? The kidnapping and your young child?" asked Intus, ears perking up a little as she jumped onto my jacket lapel—why hadn't I taken my jacket off?—and took a peek down my blood-soaked top.

"Of course! Look, I know you know just about everything that happens, or will, and yes, I remember the rules about you being unable to interfere in most of it, but if there is anything you can do to help, now is most definitely the time to do it. Anything."

Intus looked up and hopped onto my hand gripping the steering wheel tight, then used a talon to scratch at her cheek. "Er, you do know you've got small chunks of human brain down your cleavage, don't you? And that you have… um, other stuff in your hair and teeth. You need to look after yourself better, have a shower. I've got a lovely hot lava bath the kids haven't made totally gross yet if you fancy it?"

I sighed, forced myself to remain calm even though everything inside me was screaming that I was wasting valuable time and should just get out and run the rest of the way. "Like I said, busy night. Bad night. Bad life. Just answer the question. Please."

"I could… er, no, that won't work. How about… No, never mind." Intus brightened and asked, "How's the boy? Is he powerful?"

"Very. And he's gone to exchange himself for the release of his father. Oskari will destroy him, turn him into a monster."

"Oh, I don't think so. They didn't do that to you."

"I just killed more people than I can count. I am a monster. They did turn me into one."

"No, any parent would do that to save their child. That makes you a mother, not a monster."

"Does it? I'm not so sure."

"I am. Anyway, if the boy is truly powerful, as expected, er, as I already know I guess, then there is something maybe I could do."

"What? Anything. Please."

"Be right back." Intus vanished in a puff of noxious smoke then reappeared a moment later on the dash again. "My advice is to hurry," she said, ears now utterly flat against her head.

I nodded, got out the car so fast I ripped the door off the hinges, and sped down the narrow road. Thick, high hedges closed in on me like I was about to be entombed for eternity in my own worst nightmare. Intus appeared on my shoulder and had no problem holding on as I ran for all I was worth.

Like this wasn't already bad enough, she kept talking, her deep, thunderous baritone driving me to distraction, making it hard to concentrate. After a mile I began to understand that this was the point. She was doing it to stop me thinking the worst, ensuring I was unable to focus on anything but her voice.

She is annoying as hell, but showed yet again what a true friend she is that night. Not that I didn't try to throttle her every few minutes, but she's fast, and immortal, so there you go. I was still a little worked up.

Okay, frantic, just not as frantic or doing as much stupid stuff as I might have otherwise been.

Ten minutes later and the otherwise dark hills were lit up in the distance, a circle of light that left me in no doubt where this was all going to take place.

High in the mountains, away from any Regulars, my future, what remained of it, waited.

I ran faster, vision enhanced to the max. Intus babbled away in my ear and sneaked peeks down my cleavage. I was intent on one thing. Saving my family.

Getting Close

Dawn broke as I made my way through the forest, passing the clearing where this all began. The huts were still there, the fire pits too, but there was no sign of life, no hint of the death and the torture that had occurred.

I forced myself to stand still, to get a feel for the place, and sank into an almost trance-like state. With my senses opened, I felt the power of the place for the first time. Felt the meeting of powerful ley lines right at this spot, energy channeling down from the mountains and from the forests, merging like a lake of magic right here. No wonder this was where it all kicked off, where a strong veil had been put into place by those who shouldn't have had such skill. Where my son was killed and reborn.

But nobody was here now, and I didn't get it. Surely Oskari knew of this place by now, if he hadn't earlier? It was why he'd come, wasn't it? Something else was going on. I looked up to the distant mountains, and then I ran.

My speed slowed as the forest grew dense, and I surprised myself that I had sense enough to dodge trees and hidden rabbit holes and badger dens that could have ended my quest for revenge or at least delayed it. The forest was cool and damp, full of the chatter of waking birds greeting the day cheerily, but I felt no cheer, had no love of the dawn, and their song fell silent at my passing.

Even Intus finally gave up her babbling, her mood changing along with mine. As I jogged through lush undergrowth, we talked in depth about what had happened, and I realized that she may be a creature from another place, outside of time and space as we know it, but she didn't know everything that had happened. She probably hadn't been paying enough attention to events because she had kids in the hundreds to look after. I couldn't imagine such a life, such a way of being. Able to see the past, present, and future of us here on earth yet unable to interfere in much of importance.

Intus seemed content enough with the way it worked though, and I guess imps are just hardwired that way. The more I told her of what had happened, the angrier she got, and the tighter she held on to my jacket, until the leather became so torn she had to swap sides and I ran like a dog with tattered ears from too much fighting, which was exactly how I felt.

That, and absolutely disgusted with myself.

I had, and there was no getting away from it, brought my son into such a world.

But I'd beaten myself up about that enough, and I had to satisfy myself with knowing I'd also given him the most beautiful, wondrous gift of all. Life itself. Such a rare thing, the chances of it happening so remote as to be almost an impossibility, yet he was alive, and I swore I would do everything in my power to ensure he remained so. I would gladly give my life for him, and I would never, ever, let Oskari or anyone else use him for their own ends.

I smiled as I thought about that. Let them try. Nobody knew what he was like but me, what he was capable of, and I don't think I even came close to grasping the full magnitude of his powers. I doubt he did either. But he would grow, become a man, and his true strengths would be revealed. What was obvious, and maybe I'm being a bit biased here, maybe not, was that he was a good person. He had a conscience, he had depth of character and was considerate and polite. Not bad going considering how quickly he'd had to adjust to the overwhelming barrage of raw experience this world thrust upon him the moment he awoke.

I burst through the trees and stopped as I entered a clearing. The grass sparkled, green and crisp, lit by the sun's early morning rays. It was beautiful, breathtaking in its simple beauty.

"Nice spot for a picnic," noted Intus. "Don't suppose you've got any Marmite?"

"Nope, afraid not."

"Not even a bit? Have you checked all your pockets?" Intus waggled where her eyebrows would be if she had any body hair, and grinned at me, something that is a little disconcerting until you get used to seeing a mouthful of miniature rows of razor sharp teeth that run from one side of her head to the other.

"Haha, I definitely don't have even a smidge. I hate the stuff. Who the hell puts fermented yeast on their toast? It's gross."

Intus put her hands on her hips and gave me the eye. "You take that back. It's proof there is a God. It's the tastiest elixir in existence. Yum." Intus poked out her forked tongue and licked her thin lips, a massive grin getting so wide I worried it would wrap around her head. Now that would be freaky.

"What am I going to do, Intus? How am I going to save everyone?"

"I don't know if you can." She frowned, not a good look for an Imp as they are usually so happy it's infuriating. "Oskari will cheat, you know that. No way will he let anyone go, the repercussions are too great. He won't swap Faz and the others for Kane, he'll kill them."

"I know, that's why I need a plan."

"Plans, schmans, when do plans ever work out? You gotta charge in and go for it. What are you, a noob?"

"Um, actually, yes, a total noob at being an enforcer. A total noob at everything." Intus was an enforcer for the imps, one of many, what with them being such a troublesome lot.

"Oh, sorry, forgot." Intus gave me a smile again and, with nothing else coming to mind, I readied myself, then began the ascent to meet my fate and that of my family.

All Alone

"Intus?" I asked as I stepped from a deep bed of moss onto rock as I began the climb.

"Yes?"

"Does it get boring? Living forever?"

"Dunno, haven't done it yet."

I turned to my friend, and laughed. Laughed so hard I almost fell backward. "Now that is a damn good answer to an impossible to answer question. So you aren't bored, even though you've lived for, um, exactly how long has it been?"

"It's been since the start of the human race. But it's not as though you can count it in years. Our time is different to yours. There are fast bits and slow bits, all over the place really." She shrugged as if it meant little.

"How can you live like that?"

"Maybe you should be asking yourself how can humans live knowing every second, every minute, and hour is the same length. Who wants to have everything so uniform? Where's the fun in that? Life's full of surprises, and us imps do our best to make things a little more interesting for you humans."

"Don't see how hiding a hat, then putting it back where the person first looked after they've searched high and low for it is making life more interesting."

"Kate, you don't get it at all, do you?"

"Enlighten me." I was becoming interested despite myself. But this was what I needed, a distraction, so I played along.

"Because, not often, but every now and then, just occasionally, maybe the person who is looking for their hat decides to open a drawer, or root around in a box, or check a place they haven't looked for years and they find, oh, I don't know, maybe a bundle of love letters from their wife from fifty years ago."

"That would be nice."

"Right. And they spend a morning remembering all the happy years and stop moping about their quiet, lonely house and begin to look at it with fresh eyes, and it becomes a place full of joyous memories and they get a new lease on life. Maybe they don't take the tablets they were planning on taking that evening, and instead they make a phone call to one of their children and arrange to see the grandkids instead. Stuff like that." Intus shrugged. "But mostly we do it because it's loads of fun to see you guys running around cursing and you look so funny when you find stuff right where you left it."

"You, my friend, are a pretty nice imp."

"Don't tell anyone," said Intus seriously. "I mean it, I have a reputation to maintain."

"Don't worry, your secret is safe with me."

I kept on climbing, the way getting steeper, until I found a piece of flat ground and paused for a second to check my surroundings and gather myself for what was to come. As I walked forward on the uneven rock, slowly and carefully as any mistake now would be extremely bad timing, my body took the opportunity to remind me how exhausted it was.

My legs turned to jelly and a deep lethargy sprang from nowhere, threatening to pull me down into slumber. I shook my head, the wind catching my hair thick with blood and all kinds of nasties, dragging it out behind me.

Next I shook out my arms and legs, trying to wake them and remind them this was far from over. But they felt like lead weights rather than full of magical elements used to create the universe itself.

I was only human, I had to remind myself, no matter how far from Regular I was. I was still a person and people get tired, and I had just about every excuse under the sun to be less than fighting fit.

The wind really took hold and my jacket flapped about, the raggedy leather like a living creature, clinging to me then trying to escape and soar away across the treetops below.

As I stared at the trees, I noticed that some were shaking more than others, that the wind must have been ripping through the forest at an astonishing rate to disturb them like that. Guess there was a storm coming although the sky appeared clear.

I stepped out further and checked in every direction I could, and it was then I noticed the blurring shapes of what were undoubtedly vampires rushing to the summons of their Head. Stragglers, no doubt, as most vampires would already be here, amassed above with Oskari in a safe haven until this business was settled. Why not go to the clearing? Was there more energy above than below? Or maybe Oskari just wanted a vantage point to send out attack parties? So many questions.

He wouldn't know who I'd told about this, and although I doubted he was scared he would certainly have heard about what I'd done in Cardiff so would be ready for me, probably with a nasty surprise up his sleeve to keep me from doing anything I knew I wouldn't regret but he sure as hell would.

I dismissed such thoughts; whatever awaited me I would just have to deal with it. There was little else I could do unless I wanted to risk the lives of my friends back home, and enough people were already in danger.

The forest stirred again, and trees toppled, but I was so damn tired I couldn't focus properly. Intus was tugging at my earlobe and saying something.

"What?"

"I said I have to go. Some of the kids have decided it would be a good idea to play dunk Daddy in the lava bath, and it's, er, gone a bit solid. Time to get the chisel out. Again."

"Hope it all works out. Thanks, Intus, I'll see you soon. Hopefully."

"That's the spirit," she said, smiling. Then she was gone.

I was alone.

Rock tumbled behind me and I turned, knowing it wouldn't be anything fun like an avalanche.

It's Alive

For a moment I was confused by what I saw. It was as if the mountain was coming alive. It wobbled and writhed and rocks small and large tumbled and clattered from far above and all around me. I could hear the mountain below as if it was grinding its way to a new position, as if the whole mountainside was shifting like a glacier but sped up.

Trolls.

Lots, and lots, of trolls.

A living mountain of timeless beings made from the planet itself. All moving in one direction.

Up.

Toward my son.

This was what Brewster had been doing back in the grounds of the castle. Communing with his kind, telling them where to go, what had happened, who was here.

My son.

Damn, did every creature in the Hidden world want a piece of me and mine? Seemed like it.

I was shoved aside by a slice of mountain that towered above my head, three times my size. Another wild troll not seen in the cities. It made the one I'd encountered here previously seem almost like a dwarf. It grunted and strode across the ground then gripped the rock face and climbed with practiced ease, its movements orchestrated so it didn't interfere with its neighbors. The whole area was writhing with them now, hardly a piece of the rock face free of them.

Up they went, countless trolls as sure-footed as mountain goats, each foot placement and hand hold perfect, never stopping, fluid and full of grace, a sight to behold.

Why were they all here? Why was this so important? Because of Kane? Obviously. But something else maybe? Had they come to bear witness? Not content with one recording this and sharing with the others, but each of them wanting to see it with their own eyes and lock it forever as a part of history in their priceless quartz brains?

This was overwhelming. What had begun as a fight for personal survival and to save my family and friends was becoming something altogether more epic. And frightening. What on earth was this all about? Would they help me? Would they save Kane, save Faz and the others? Or would they stand idly by and watch as Oskari obliterated everything I held dear?

I dashed to the steep rock face and began to climb but I kept getting pushed aside by the trolls. I wasn't part of the orchestrated movements and it seemed they didn't consider anything organic to be of that much importance.

I wanted to scream at them, ask them if they knew who I was and what part I had to play in this, but they refused to look at me, refused to answer when I asked, even when I insulted them.

So, unable to get past them, unable to think what else to do and how to climb without getting squashed, I launched myself onto the shoulders of the biggest, baddest, most colorful troll I could see, hung on around his neck and said, "Mind if I hitch a ride?"

His head turned and he stared at me, then grunted, faced the rock, and continued his climb.

It beat getting flattened, and boy can they move faster than you'd think when they've got some place they want to be in a hurry.

Here We Go Again

From the rate of ascent, I could only assume trolls were either a lot happier, and speedier, climbing than walking, or something had lit a fire under their hard asses and they'd pulled out all the stops.

It was probably a bit of both.

We reached the halfway point after traversing precipitous outcrops I believed impassable, went over huge jutting crags without a pause, and circumnavigated to the other side without a single one of them slowing or putting a limb wrong.

Pebbles and boulders crashed down on those beneath but they ignored the missiles, kept their heads down, and continued climbing. Which was all well and good for those below, but not so good for me, as I am not made of rock, and I am very much able to be squashed and broken into bony bits by large lumps of hard stuff slamming into my head.

The longer we climbed, the lower I got on the trolls back as I tried to shield myself from the increasingly hostile environment. My grip was weakening, my worry was increasing, and my cuts were multiplying. I pumped magic furiously out from my body to form a shield just a few millimeters thick to save energy, but shields had never been my strong point and the state I was in made it almost impossible to maintain.

When I felt like I couldn't hold on or protect myself for a moment longer, I found myself hanging from the thick back muscles of the troll, his body motionless. I glanced down, surprised to discover we were on flat ground, and thankfully let go. Landing in a cloud of dust, I coughed, ignored the wobble in my legs, and stood. To say it was cramped is a real understatement. Everywhere I could see, and granted that wasn't very far as I was basically standing in a forest of giants, were trolls, trolls, and more trolls.

Big ones, little ones, jet black ones, others white as chalk, some with luminous striations of crystals running across their bodies in amazing patterns, this was like a gathering of every possible style of troll there was. And once on this wide, mostly level part of the mountain, they stood completely still, saying nothing.

I moved between them, ducking under legs, clambering over bodies, until they were so hard pressed to each other that I apologized quietly then clambered up one and took to walking across the shoulders of the amassed crowd like it was a second story. Nobody objected, nobody moved or said a word.

They were communicating, I was sure of it. A silent, intense energy passing between them as they shared information and maybe even planned their next move. Would it involve squashing all the nasty vampires, except me and Kane of course? I certainly hoped so. Or would they simply be picking their spot, like booking a seat at the cinema, organizing themselves so they got a good view of whatever show awaited? Sure to be a real surprise. I was at a loss.

The ground rose and the way became uneven as I hopped from shoulder to shoulder. It was a good few minutes before I ran out of trolls and found myself standing above the crowd looking down on thousands of hard heads. What a sight, something never before seen by any human alive as far as I knew.

A shudder ran through the crowd like the wind was sweeping their thoughts in a single direction. Then they were on the move without warning. There were no orders given, no direction spoken of, nothing but a shift from stationary to moving. Away from me and toward the source of light I'd seen from far below.

The forest was lost to me now, hidden by the shape of the mountain, only the distant land visible.

"Wait, what are you doing here? Will you help?"

None of them paid me any attention, gave an encouraging word, or acknowledged me in any way.

"Screw you then." I shouted, then ran after them, putting on a burst of speed and traversing the rock as fast as I could.

I caught up with those in front within a minute and looked ahead but there was little to see, certainly not a vampire in sight....Yet.

Stop, Start

Every few minutes the group paused and became so immobile I lost track of what was troll and what was mountain. It was surreal and I swear I began to believe I was making the whole thing up, that I was delirious and alone on the mountain simply imagining things.

Then they'd move as one and I'd be assured they were really here, until the next time it happened. I was at the front of the troll horde now, keeping pace with the fastest, and the landscape of the mountain changed again. The terrain evened out, going from crags and large overhangs, huge boulders and switchbacks, or perilous climbs, to large swathes of open space where the ground was flat and my bloodied hands had opportunity to repair until the next short climb and more ripping of fingers and more spilling of blood.

My jacket was barely hanging on me now, ripped by rocks, snagged and pulled free so many times it hung in ribbons. My trousers were the same, the knees worn through, torn in numerous places. I didn't even want to think what my bum looked like, as I'd done a lot of sliding over a lot of sharp rock, and judging by the wind chill at my posterior there was definitely something unladylike happening back there. I just hoped I'd worn nice underwear, but for the life of me I couldn't remember what I'd put on, if anything. Trying to feel for signs of modesty was pointless, my fingers were so numb and ragged that all sensation was gone.

Suddenly the lead team stopped, and the sound of an army coming to a halt behind told me their numbers had increased. I glanced back and boy were there a lot of them now, more than I'd imagined. A solid wall of sentient stone all acting like a single being. The leaders pumped their fists in the air, and so did the army, and then a loud bellow issued from their mouths, deafening me. It echoed around the mountains, through valleys, down to the forests far below, shaking trees and scaring wildlife.

Then they ran.

I mean really ran.

And I am small and they were very big. So I jumped on the nearest pair of shoulders again and got taken for the ride of a lifetime.

Eek!

"Stop, stop!" I shouted, utterly freaked out.

I glanced at the solid wall of rock several strides in front of us, me now unfortunately on the lead troll, and at the mass of rampaging trolls behind us. If I tried to jump down I'd be flattened and my mad vamp skills wouldn't save me. But if I stayed where I was I would be flattened anyway.

What was a girl to do?

I closed my eyes, that's what. And I prayed that these dumb brutes who watched over humanity yet never, ever interfered, knew something I didn't. Like, how to smash through mountains.

The roar of the wind was replaced with a familiar sensation, that of passing from one plane to another. A place that was no place, a realm that was no realm, neither on earth nor anywhere else. A supernatural, truly Hidden place.

Shifting feet stopped behind me, the collective sound a sharp crunch as thousands of trolls broke through to the other side and halted just out of unison. In a second they must have all been through as everything went deathly silent and I deigned to open my somewhat damp eyes.

"Huh?" It wasn't just dark, there was zero light. I had to put my fingers to my eyes to check they were open, which was a terrible idea as my fingers were still numb. My eyeballs weren't though, and as I poked myself and let out a squeal, I knew this couldn't be good.

Why had they rushed through the mountain into somewhere utterly devoid of even a hint of light? Why had they been in such a hurry if this was what they were after? Did they have a special watching room like the dwarves that we'd march off to next? Or did they just want to get out of the wind and somehow observe what happened to my family from a distance?

I dared not get off the troll's shoulders as I had no idea how close the others were or what would happen if I did. For all I knew they'd be off running at solid walls again within a heartbeat and I didn't want to be crushed, not now, not ever.

Something made the troll I was hitching a ride on stir, and he turned, so did the others judging by the sounds. I thought I could make out a pinprick of light ahead but it could have just been the effects of poking myself in the eye. I blinked several times but it remained, and it got slowly closer. It took a long time, almost a minute, for it to get close enough for me to realize it was a flame. Burning bright and flickering ever so slightly in the gentle draughts that came from places I couldn't see, only understanding that this space was vast to house so many trolls and for the light to have been so distant.

Another minute and everything came into focus, the light a flame on the end of a long torch held out in front of the oldest dwarf I'd ever seen, and I don't think any of those you see are particularly young, not by human standards anyway. The face was wrinkled like paper scrunched up then flattened out a bit, the hair was white, tinged with ash, and hung in a braid just above the ground. His beard was just as long, and both swished to and fro as he walked with strong, powerful legs toward us.

Had to give it to the guy, he had a serious set of dwarf balls.

He stopped in front of us and frowned, bushy eyebrows meeting in the middle. He adjusted a heavy broadsword tucked into his belt and said in a gruff voice, "This way. Everyone's waiting."

With that he turned and strode away.

The trolls moved as one, and I went with them.

Damn Dwarves

The sound of thousands upon thousands of feet stomping on perfectly polished rock is not something I'm likely to ever forget. It was hypnotic and terrifying. A tectonic shift was occurring inside the mountain and it felt unstoppable.

Every single troll walked in unison, slow to keep pace with the hurrying yet still regal bearing of the lead dwarf, yet still faster than they'd ever moved back home. The trolls were focused, intent on whatever the end game to all this was, and I was along for the ride. Yet I got the feeling this was more about me and mine than it was about them, so couldn't quite understand why I was being dismissed as someone without even a bit part in this epic drama.

And anyway, what the hell was happening? Why were we in the realm of the dwarves again? I couldn't be sure, but I was kinda certain this was the same area we'd visited previously, not far from the Looking Room although distance was all relative in these places. On and on we marched, still in the same vast space, it seemingly never ending. Then the dwarf's torch cast an orange glow on a wall with a tunnel mouth twenty feet high and we followed without missing a step, without him turning and acknowledging us in any way.

I entered first, or the troll did and I ducked and wrapped my arms tight around his massive neck, surprisingly comfortable perched on his wide shoulders, his thick back muscles—I know, they aren't really muscles as they're made of rock—acting like a pad for my battered bottom.

In single file we followed the torchlight, us close enough for me to see that the curved tunnel walls were covered in intricate markings and abstract patterns that ran in continuous lines down the whole length. They were typical dwarven style, gentle curves and fat knots, woven lines that flowed past symbols of axes and hammers and always the irregular lumps of gold, beautiful and carved by artists who'd spent hundreds of years perfecting their craft.

I'd seen these carvings before, but not on this scale. It was almost like they meant more than they did at first glance, as though they were telling me something I couldn't decipher. As if the lines were leading somewhere of terrible significance and I was too far removed from the culture to understand where I was headed or the true import of this.

The lead dwarf and the trolls seemed to understand what was happening though, were acting as if we were somewhere holy. Maybe we were. Maybe he was taking us all to pray. Or maybe he was taking us to the bowels of Hell itself and I'd be thrown into a fiery pit of eternal damnation for my sins that were accruing more rapidly by the hour.

Maybe I deserved nothing less.

The tunnel was perfectly straight, did not deviate in any way, yet there was no light at the end that I could see, just more of the same. The further we walked, the more intense the patterns became, everything taking on a jagged edge, the sweeping lines turning angry, barbed with thorns and the semi-abstract imagery becoming increasingly violent. Color was implemented, and rather than the work being straight carvings into the rock the patterns were stained with minerals.

It began with blues and yellows, as if representing the outside world. Calm colors morphed into garish purple, then red and orange, fierce colors and random striations like the walls had been slashed and were bleeding, the patterns finally interrupted. Then the flow broke until everything turned nightmarish, the beauty replaced with more and more weaponry, shapes that could be humanoid if you squinted and used your imagination a little.

Long lines bisected the figures in endless configurations, splitting heads and slicing limbs, innards spilled only to begin new patterns that meandered to the next victim where bodies were sliced in two and large axes were carved in realistic ways that made me want to reach out and grab one just so I felt like I stood a chance of defending myself.

Finally it all fell apart in a spectacular way.

The dwarf stopped at the end of the tunnel, facing a solid wall. The patterns from the wall and ceiling converged, then erupted in fiery bursts of bright splatters of pigment, breaking into pieces a representation of the sun, burned reddish brown with jagged edges. In the center of all this madness was a simple eye. No color, just black and white, yet all the more freaky because of it.

I had no idea what it signified, but the knot in my stomach told me it was nothing good, that I was not about to be reunited with my family so we could all go home and have a nice cuppa in the kitchen.

This was a serious business for the dwarves, the trolls too, and this bloody eye staring into my soul and freaking me out was screaming at me but I couldn't understand what it was saying.

With a sound like thunder in an enclosed space, the wall slid slowly to the right, revealing more darkness, more emptiness.

I somehow understood that this next space was larger than the last, that this was a truly vast place we'd been led to. I tried to use my enhanced vision, but as before I got nothing. Something about the spaces negated any magic I could use to see better, so the only light was that of the dwarf's, and all he revealed in the next room was a polished rock floor.

He began to walk. We followed.

I considered jumping down and running off, but where to?

I could still see that eye, it was imprinted in my mind and I did not like what it was doing to my insides. They were squirming like they wanted to pop out of my belly button and crawl away, and that couldn't be good, right?

Dumped

The dwarf turned and acknowledged me for the first time. He nodded, holding my gaze, then turned his head and blew out the flame with powerful lungs. The after-effects of the light lingered for a second or two then I was in total darkness, and before I had chance to ask where the light switch was, the troll lifted me off his shoulders with massive, yet surprisingly gentle hands and placed me down carefully on the ground.

I dared not move, didn't know what was expected of me but knew I was meant to stand still. I felt as much as heard the trolls move, a shifting of air currents and a slow, steady rumble vibrating through the rock. It went on for several minutes yet I knew they were still in the room. Just how big was this place? Their movements became more distant until the only sound was the beating of my heart.

Should I call out? Should I walk? Should I try to run? Haha, like there was anywhere to run. And besides, this was the end game, of that I was sure.

Whatever was going to go down, and go down it would, this was where it all led. Why, I had no idea. What any of this was about was a mystery, but here I was, and here I would remain until someone told me different.

A light appeared far, far away, so I shrugged, and walked.

I cannot begin to describe the feeling of moving through absolute darkness toward a single spot of light many minutes distant when you know there are thousands of pairs of eyes belonging to trolls, and whatever else was out there, tracking your progress because they could see in this blackness. My footsteps echoed strangely, the sound bouncing off the bodies I knew were amassed, but never reaching the end of the place I was in.

My footsteps were steady and confident though, I forced myself to neither run nor dawdle, but to own it. Keeping up the pace, forcing confidence I did not feel into my steps, actually helped settle nerves I thought had left long ago. Truth be told, I was very scared, and it took a lot to scare me now. I followed the light, keeping my head up high and my shoulders back, although if anyone was staring at the gaping hole at my rear, one cheek feeling like it was poking out the ripped leather, I'm sure the effect would have been somewhat tarnished.

Whatever, let them look. Trolls didn't go in for firm yet wobbly female bottoms anyway, but still, it kind of hurt my pride.

Minute after minute I walked, and then I was only a handful of paces from the light. It was a simple torch like the dwarf's, left lying on the ground, burning steadily with a definite tang of something animal judging by the strong odor and smoke it emitted.

It lit only several feet of rocky ground, but I kept going, and only stopped once I was within the ring of brightness. As I did, quieter footsteps from the other side of the fire approached and my heart leaped. I may not have heard them often, but I'd recognize them anywhere.

I leapt the flame and hugged my son so tight.

"You're alive! Thank God."

"Hello, Mother. Quite an adventure, isn't it?"

I released my bear hug and we stood holding hands, illuminated by the light. He looked fine, he looked calm and in control, a slight knowing smile on his face. "What happened? You shouldn't have run off like that."

"Sorry, but I had to try. I found the clearing, then this horde of trolls swept me up and then a dwarf led me here."

"Same for me. Hell, there must be thousands and thousands of trolls in here then. What are they playing at?"

"I think I know." Kane smiled at me, not in a happy way, but in a, ooh, this is gonna be epic, and probably far from nice, way.

"Think maybe you want to share?"

"They're fed up with us."

"Who, the trolls?"

"Um, not just them. I think it's the dwarves too. And, er, maybe some others, not sure."

"How'd you mean?"

"I mean look at all the madness we create. Humans I mean. Maybe they want to teach us a lesson?"

I thought for a moment, but it didn't feel right. "No, this is just behavior as usual, I'm afraid. It's because of you."

"Why would the trolls or the dwarves care about me?"

"I have absolutely no idea. But I think we're going to find out. Did you see the vampires? Did you see your father?"

"Not up close, just lots of vampires in the distance, then the trolls came."

I squeezed Kane's hands and tried to reassure him, but I doubt it helped him much as I wasn't exactly feeling full of confidence myself. "Don't worry, I'm sure everything will be fine."

Famous last words, right?

Time to Say Urgle

Something huge, and undoubtedly heavy, scraped across the ground. How I imagined it must be if you're stuck between two continents sliding past each other. Rock pulverizing, coastlines smashing, that kind of thing.

Wind roared through the opening for a moment, but there was no way to know where it was or how large it truly was. The flame at our feet was snuffed out and we held each other tight as thousands upon thousands of new lights appeared like stars in the night sky, all moving slowly from just off-center of where we faced. They were too distant to give any sign of who was carrying them, more a hint of light than making a difference to the overwhelming darkness. Then the sound came again and with it more wind, and then a final thud that closed the opening. The lights vanished.

Darkness again.

We stood there, both of us rigid, but I could tell Kane had his back straight and his shoulders squared just like his mum.

Without warning, and I really would have liked some, everything was bathed in dwarven light. It was everywhere and nowhere, illuminating the vast space with no visible sign of its source. Not that I took any time to ponder such things anyway, I was focusing on the hordes of trolls and dwarves that had amassed.

We stood at the center of a circle with a hundred meter diameter, and then, and I have to hand it to them, it was pretty well orchestrated, ten thousand dwarves encircled us, each dressed in full battle regalia. Meaning, they wore their usual clothes consisting of lots of leather, plenty of chain mail, and more weapons than was probably strictly necessary, plus requisite hammers and chisels and bags for any gold they might happen to find.

Ranked behind them, stretching as far as I could see, and I could see a long way now, were trolls. Countless trolls. It was impossible to tell how many as they simply kept on going, all the colors of the earth and its bounty, quartz and salts and minerals and everything ever found beneath the earth formed in, over, or around their rock bodies, some sparkling, some as dark as coal. From average, to the truly impressive ones you never met as they were too massive to belong anywhere but in the dark places and the high mountains far away from humanity.

It felt like the entire world population of trolls had descended on this place, but I knew that couldn't have been true as how could they have arrived so quickly? But then I realized they could have, because if the dwarves allowed them to use their endless passages and places where the borders between worlds became blurred, then spanning continents became as easy as crossing the street.

Everyone was still, all eyes were on us, and it was very difficult not to run screaming, except the only thing I'd run into was an axe.

Kane turned to me, much calmer than I was, and said, "Is it often like this, Mother?" He seemed amused, like he wanted to chuckle, and as his smile spread so did mine despite myself, until I couldn't control it any longer and I laughed until my belly hurt because of the sheer ridiculousness of the whole thing.

He joined me, because it was one of those contagious laughs that you couldn't help but find hilarious, and when we'd laughed ourselves dry I answered my son. "Not normally, no. This is, um, pretty unique, even for me."

"It makes being alive very interesting," noted Kane. "I'm glad you had me."

"So am I." With his words I felt a world of suffering, doubt, self-recrimination, and self-hate lift. Whatever happened, I'd done the right thing by bringing my beautiful boy into this world. Were there things I would change if I could? You betcha. But he was here, I was here, and he had seen such wonders to make any Hidden envious.

I lifted my head, wiped my eyes, and addressed the room in general. "Okay, enough games. What's this about?"

The dwarf who had guided our way stepped forward directly in front of us and paused after several steps. "It's about the future. The future of us all." There were murmurs of agreement from dwarf and troll alike. "This has gone on long enough. Today it gets settled. We either remain a part of your world, or we retreat to our own and never return. Today it will be decided."

"I don't understand." I didn't, I really didn't.

"Your Council is laughable. They allow some of your kind to kill indiscriminately. Kill the Regulars, and do nothing. They contradict your own morality, your own Laws. All our Laws. The time has finally come for there to be a change. Either the Hidden world is reset, the world where we interact with humans, or we no longer play a part in it. It is up to you."

He was looking straight at me. Was he confused? Was he out of his mind? "Do you mean my son? He's the one everyone seems to think is a prophet. Which I assure you he is not. I'm just his mother."

"No, I mean you. This. Ends. Now."

And before I could argue, or ask more questions, like how the hell he expected me to do anything about the countless vampires throughout the world who killed innocents, the way behind him parted and revealed, not one, not two, but several thousand vampires. Every vampire that had departed before I ran riot in the city.

So this was what the dwarf was talking about. He expected me to kill them all, destroy them and set something else in motion.

If he did, then he would be severely disappointed. I was strong, and Kane more so, but there were limits. Hell, Oskari had crucified me. I didn't stand a chance fighting just him, let alone thousands of my kind.

Then I saw Faz held in Oskari's tight grip as the vampires got closer, and then Dancer and Persimmon held fast by others, and the fear in Mithnite's eyes, and I decided, fuck it, I'd give it a good go.

Rough Around the Edges

Oskari stopped at the front of the crowd, directly in line with the dwarves. It wasn't that it looked like he particularly wanted to, it was the dwarves barring his way with axes that made him halt. He snarled at them but stopped nonetheless. Even he knew it was a bad idea to piss off that many dudes with weapons, let alone the thousands of trolls there as back-up to ensure nobody did anything unsanctioned.

The way parted after the dwarf in charge whispered in Oskari's ear. The Head nodded and released Faz. Persimmon, Dancer, and Mithnite were also freed. Dwarves shifted aside until there was a large space for the vampires to spread out, and spread out they did. They ended up standing in a line fifty wide, Oskari at the center. Row after row were behind, all looking pissed off, rightfully scared, and probably wishing they could go home.

I didn't care, I only had eyes for Faz. He looked rough, but he was in one piece, and his suit had held up remarkably well considering he'd obviously been through the wringer. Dancer and Persimmon were in similar condition, ruffled but no sign of any serious wounds, just bruises and dirt on their clothes, maybe a tear here or there. Mithnite was hardly touched, but the way he moved told me he'd had no easy ride.

Faz rubbed at his arm and took in what faced him before his eyes locked on mine. Electricity ran through my body and I saw him shudder like he felt the same thing. It was only then I really understood the deep connection we had with each other, forged through love, pain, excitement, more than our fair share of sorrow, magic, death, murder, and lots of laughs and cringe-inducing quips on his part.

He stepped forward cautiously, probably because he expected to be stopped, but Oskari didn't move and neither did any vampire. Mithnite joined Faz and then Persimmon and Dancer were on the move too. Then I was moving, Kane's hand still in mine, until we were embracing. My heart leaped for joy. Faz broke from me and turned to Kane.

"You've grown," he said, like he knew exactly what had been happening.

"Hello, Father, nice to meet you."

"You too, Son." Faz pulled Kane to him and hugged him tight. I saw him sag, saw the tension drop from his body, and the energy surge with renewed hope. Faz would do anything to save his son, same as I would.

This was not over. Not by a long shot.

"What happened? How are you, er, like this?" asked Faz.

"Long story, Father. The vampires are to blame, but um, I am one too."

"What!?" Faz turned and I flinched. I couldn't help it, I began to cry.

"I tried to stop it, to stop him, but we were about to be killed and…"

"I'm not angry." Faz frowned and his jaw clenched as he turned and said, "I'm going to kill you," as he stared at Oskari. Oskari didn't even flinch. He was one cool customer under pressure.

"No, I am," I said, and I damn well meant it.

Before we all had the chance to even say much of anything else, the dwarf marched up to us and said, "Now there are two sides. I assume you're enemies of the vampires who would kill innocents?"

We agreed, we all always had, but even Dancer was unable to stop them, was controlled by the Council he himself ran for our country, and much as he hated it he didn't have the manpower to even attempt to stop their deadly, but usually covert feeding.

"Then it begins!" the dwarf bellowed.

Dwarves and trolls closed in, pushing the vampires forward, and then it was them and us.

Only problem being, them and us was us six against several thousand very pissed off vampires led by the deadliest Head the country had ever known.

Stacked Odds

Once the vampires had been directed forward, the circle of dwarves and trolls backed up to accommodate them. There were more than I'd thought. Way more. No way could we fight them and win. We were gonna be obliterated. The vampires amassed where they'd been herded, forty or fifty deep, going back row after row, with Oskari at the head. Once the others had retreated, they spread out forming a large semi-circle, acting in unison, directed by Oskari's will.

I felt it pushing at my mind as he tried to force himself on me. Kane grunted and shook his head as if to dislodge a gnat and then he nodded at me.

Oskari emitted a low grumble of anger and frustration then removed his glasses. His cold eyes burned with hatred. There also a deep, almost uncontrollable lust. Not for the joys of the flesh, but for the anticipation of power. Part of him wanted Kane to resist his advances, for it proved just how useful he was.

Oskari craved my son, desired and coveted him even more as his awareness of what he was capable of grew. I saw no way that he wouldn't get exactly what he wanted.

"How are you feeling?" I asked Faz.

"A bit beat up, but could be worse," he said, smiling in that familiar, cheeky way I've always found so endearing and so damn sexy.

"You back on fighting form?"

Faz shifted and fidgeted with his hands but held my gaze without blinking and said, "Good enough to give these jokers a proper hiding."

"No holds barred?"

Faz nodded, face draining of all humor, and said, "No holds barred." Magic crackled from his entire body as his ink fattened, black fractal shards of potent death that made it impossible to tell where his dark suit ended and his powers began. His eyes snapped to black as we gazed at each other and he turned from the lovable rogue so many know to the killing machine few have ever witnessed and survived.

Copying my lover's cue, my own eyes snapped to a dark emptiness so fast and hard it made me gasp. My teeth snicked down, drawing blood from my lower lip and I licked it, the power it contained sending my body into a spiral of craving and bloodlust that set every nerve, every sense, alight. I expanded and became animal. Wild, full of desire. Dangerous.

"Let's do this," said Dancer eagerly, having clearly felt impotent being unable to fight back against the vampires for so long. His own eyes hardened and changed color, something I had never seen, and purple swirls of danger cocooned his body.

Persimmon smiled a beautiful smile. Her pert, full bosom heaved in mesmerizing fashion and I caught Kane gulp at the sight. Then her skin exploded though her clothes, her butterscotch flesh exposed as she dropped to all fours, naked and beautiful even as she twisted and cracked as she shifted into a sleek panther that was as perfect as her.

"Cool," whispered Kane. His eyes widened at the sight of Persimmon's transformation and he too dropped to all fours. My son's youthful body stretched and popped as bone metamorphosed and his skin darkened. Fur grew as his head widened and his ears elongated. Then there were two sleek, lithe panthers side by side. Persimmon tilted her head to him and made a low purring noise, Kane responded in kind.

He nodded his head on thick muscles as he blinked and his eyes became dark, empty of emotion. Then, as the assembled masses gasped at his show of power, he faced the vampires and hissed. Large canines snicked down hard and fast, a sound that filled the space and silenced the vampires. They were the longest set of deadly fangs anyone had ever seen, and they belonged to my son.

I wanted to weep.

Oskari's eyes widened in surprise and then he smiled as his own teeth dropped down hard and deadly. Following his cue, the entire surviving population of Cardiff vampires let their own fangs be revealed. The sound of so many pairs of deadly teeth is not something any mother wants to hear.

"You can't have him," I said, voice flat.

"You're a dead man," growled Faz as he raised his hands.

"The boy is mine," whispered Oskari, his voice dripping with desire. He raised long, perfectly manicured fingers then dropped his hand.

The vampires roared, charging forward.

Power Unleashed

In the split-second before the vampires rushed us, I suddenly remembered why everything was happening here. Oskari had retreated to this part of the country—although technically we weren't in Snowdonia anymore we kinda still were—because of the power of the converging ley lines. We'd been set up from the beginning to come here so Kane could be taken and his metamorphosis started. Oskari knew there was immense power here, that there was something different about it, that all energy would be enhanced and he stood a better chance of getting what he wanted, but what about us?

In his arrogant way, he would have given it hardly a thought, knowing I was young and inexperienced and that he had vast knowledge of all things magical even if he wasn't a practitioner himself. As with most vamps, he relied on the power of blood, but if he'd come here then he wanted, and could channel, the forces running through this site. Did it still work in the dwarven realm? Was it still a potent place?

I allowed myself to search for the strong currents of magical forces I'd felt above the surface in the real world, but they were lacking here. This place was too alien for humans, too apart from our world of familiar magic. We were, when you got right down to it, on our own. The battle would be fought with the power we had inside, with what we could muster and control, no extra help given.

Oh, how he must have been disappointed when he was captured. That his advantage was lost, that somewhere he'd believed would allow him to take the next step of the vampires' evolution was taken from him. Yet he still had his backup, and was confident he would win. After all, why wouldn't he? He had thousands, we were few, and the dwarves and trolls seemed content to let us fight this out amongst ourselves.

So be it. If there was no extra power to be drawn from the land itself, then I'd make do with what I had inside.

"Ready?" I asked Faz as I steadied my stance and let a calmness wash over me.

"Damn straight." Faz grinned, cocked his head, and gave the running vampires a sneer. I loved him for it, for him facing down death in his "fuck-you" attitude, and it gave me hope.

"You and me," I said, and we both had the same thought at the same time.

We grabbed hands, forming a fist so tight it was like our bone and flesh fused. As our ink activated fully, and magic channeled through our bodies, a barrier was torn asunder and the Hidden powers of a young vampire and a century-old wizard combined in a frenzy of manic mayhem.

As one, we directed our magic, until there was no me and him, no individual strength or weakness, only a single, deadly and unbelievably violent power source that almost knocked us unconscious.

For a moment I wavered, then I gritted my teeth, gave myself to it totally, and was consumed by the man I loved so very much and the magic I both loathed and worshiped. My true addiction. My love, my hate, my sense of violence and source of bottomless love for the men in my life.

Our joined fist rose as the vampires charged, and before the others could join the attack and get taken down, our hands glowed white hot. Magic backed up in our systems, pressure building until it spat from our sign of trust and love in a spasming burst of fury that threw us back ten feet onto our asses and obliterated the first few rows of our attackers. I don't mean just knocked them down and broke a few bones, I mean totally obliterated.

The room fell silent, all movement stopped as the vampires behind the front rows stared down at the ash-covered ground. They were gone. Several hundred vampires had vanished as if they'd never been. All that remained was a light covering of ash; more fell and drifted lazily around the silent cavern.

Faz and I rushed to our feet, the connection lost, and I knew that was it, that we could never recreate such a feat. We were ourselves once more, individuals with only the power as was our right, and although it cemented our bond in a way that remains, it would never be repeated.

Not ones to stand about while your enemy recovers, Persimmon and Kane sprang into action simultaneously. Two black blurs of claw-tipped death, and more teeth than was friendly, tore through the vampires while they stood gawping at what remained of their kind.

Tens fell while they recovered their sense, then the screams and the wails rose. Fists flew and fangs tried to bite but the panthers were fast and perfect for this kind of combat. They darted in and out, clawed and raked and slashed and chewed, ravaged flesh and snapped Achilles heels, ripped out throats and disemboweled before the vampires could do anything remotely effective.

Dancer joined the fray as Faz and I ran forward, but even though I would not stop, would not rest for a minute, I knew that however much of a good beginning we'd had we were still vastly outnumbered and you simply did not win against these odds.

So much sadness, so terrible that it would end like this. That most of the time I'd had with Kane was full of violence, that I'd had no time to cuddle up with Faz and make fun of his stupid shoes, that we'd never get the vegetable plots finished and a million other minor details that suddenly seemed to take on so much more importance than all this crap we got ourselves involved in.

There would be no days when we'd stay up past midnight fretting when Kane came home late, no mornings sitting around the table talking as a family. No playing in the garden, no eating dinner together, no trips to the zoo, none of that.

It ended here and now, but we were a family of fighters, and if that was the way it was to end then we wouldn't make it easy for the buggers.

Then I had an idea.

An Interruption

The problem with good ideas is that they're hard to implement when you've got a horde of fanatical, homicidal vampires attacking you. They were on us in a heartbeat, their fury and bloodlust overwhelming their fear. The panthers continued to leap and attack, then dodge and retreat, but it was a losing battle. As the vamps reached us, Faz let loose and began, as he would say, blasting the dark arts.

Black lightning sprang from his fingertips as he struck his dashing poses and kept his cool even under such extreme duress. Scores died as he sank deeper into the zone, but they kept on advancing. Dancer, not usually one to use magic in fights as his skills lay elsewhere, nonetheless let rip with an intensity and ferocity I'd never believed him capable of. He slashed through the rows as he swept his arms back and forth like he was wielding a flame thrower.

Bodies dropped, sliced through by his magic, and Mithnite, who had been uncharacteristically slow to let the Empty consume him—maybe because he was smart and didn't want to act until he was ready so he could fight longer—suddenly snapped to magic-mode and took out lone attackers one after the other with precise, directed hits that exploded heads and covered the crowd with gore.

As bones splintered and brains blew apart, I became consumed with a rage that erupted through my fingers in an uncontrollable and mindless fury. It was unstoppable and impossibly volatile, pop, pop, popping from my fingers in small and large blobs of searing, multicolored hate that blasted through row after row of our enemy as they surged forward and dodged their falling, screaming, half-obliterated comrades.

Vampires writhed on the ground, screaming or gasping. Some were repairing within moments, others were too injured to do anything but stare at me with hate-filled eyes before they met the final death.

On and on we went, giving it all we had, more magic than I thought possible coming from us in various ways. I blasted continually, burned through bodies until I finally lost power. I paused, felt energy return, and went at it again. But after several seconds I felt the power wane, knew I couldn't keep on going like this, and it was obvious the others were faring much worse. Soon they'd be writhing on the ground, paying with pain for their thievery. Kane and I wouldn't have to pay such a price, but there were limits to our reserves and they were being eaten up fast. Persimmon was also slowing, not enough to be killed yet, but it was only a matter of time.

It was now or never.

As Persimmon and Kane fell back into line to gain a brief respite, and Dancer and Faz sprayed the vampires with death, I dashed forward, grabbed them both, and dragged them back. Mithnite caught my eye and I nodded; he retreated, clearly happy to take a rest.

For a moment it was a standoff. The vampires gathered themselves, many less than keen to continue as the piles of bodies were certainly enough to make you think twice about being in the front row, and we all stood in a line facing them, chests heaving, magic fizzling, yet still consumed by the violence.

We had seconds before Faz, Mithnite, and Dancer would be unable to continue. Dancer may have passed the point in his career where he had to pay much in dues for his thievery from the Empty, but this was extreme use and I knew he'd suffer along with the others.

"Still time to make a choice," I shouted, trying to keep my voice steady. "You heard the dwarf. This is crunch time. You either change, only kill those who truly deserve it, or you die. My son will decimate you. There will be no second chance, no reprieve. You accept this or you die." I turned to Kane, and said, "Show them."

Kane nodded then morphed from panther to human. Then he was me, then Faz, then he was Oskari. The vampires gasped at the extent of Kane's abilities.

Oskari approached, his clothes pristine, hair perfect. "He is powerful, no doubt, but he belongs with us. We are vampire, we have a right to feed. You are a disgrace." He moved back to his own kind, eyes locked on mine.

There were murmurs of agreement, but it wasn't exactly unanimous. I knew many were faltering, that faced with their own mortality they would choose life over the freedom they'd grown accustomed to. But most were resolute, and they knew they could take us. They were also loyal, and I suppose that was about their only good point.

Nobody spoke and the crowd tensed. This wasn't working, this would never work.

But then someone stepped forward, pushed through the crowd. He dashed across the divide and came to us. A young man, one I knew, one I'd believed was good underneath. He nodded at me once then turned.

"We are vampire, but we don't have to lose our humanity. We can feed as Kate does, use our gifts to destroy those who are truly evil. We can do good, not bad. We can change, make the name vampire respected, not just feared."

There were insults and childish jeers, but the crowd shifted and it was clear this guy was not alone. More took hesitant steps, then ran, fearing their comrades would cut them down. Some did fall, caught before they could cross, but as the vampires fought amongst themselves many took the opportunity to come to our side until we must have been a hundred strong and maybe even stood a fighting chance.

"Game on, bitches," I shouted.

Taking Sides

Kane moved, but before I could reach him Faz grabbed his arm in a grip I knew he couldn't shake off easily. Even over the roar of battle cries I heard Faz say, "Wait here, Son. We've got a lot of catching up to do, and I don't want to be talking to a corpse."

"But, Father, I am stronger than them."

"Maybe, but there's more of them, and anyway, I'm your dad. Do as you're told."

Kane smiled at Faz, and although I saw his desire to fight, to remain a part of this and do his bit, he also understood the love behind the words. "Yes, Father."

Faz grinned like a loon and then they hugged quickly. Kane moved back and nodded at me. I smiled at him, felt so much love for my men I wanted to scream it to the world. Then a horde of vampires came charging at me and I dashed off with them following before I got crushed.

Dancer and Mithnite went down under a barrage of bodies only for the vampires to be hurled off a moment later as a torrent of colorful magic boomed. They both got up but looked truly awful, and trust me, Dancer never looks good at the best of times. Mithnite staggered and a vampire sped at him, fangs bared. No, I wouldn't have another man I loved turned, or worse, and I cut that guy down with a fist to the face that went right through.

Mithnite sagged and I knew he was spent. Dancer dropped too.

It was carnage on a scale I'd never witnessed, and it had been a gruesome few days, but this wasn't over. Faz and I protected our friends as Persimmon whipped back and forth taking out anyone that came too close. The vampires on our side formed a protective ring, another layer of defense, and the odds evened out quickly. Those who'd joined us had a hell of a lot more to lose than just their lives. They would face Oskari's wrath if they lost, so they fought with an intensity that could not be matched by those who opposed us.

More and more of Oskari's army attacked but they were either beaten down by the good vamps—never thought I'd say that—or those who managed to burst through the cordon were easily taken out by us. I blasted, Faz blasted, Persimmon raked and bit and each time this happened the opposition grew less certain of themselves and their attacks more feeble.

Oskari was shouting and cajoling, pouring scorn on those who had betrayed him, threatening punishments too innumerable and terrible to repeat, but he saw what I saw, and the worse it got for him the more incensed he became. Spittle flew from his mouth as he cursed us all, his words morphing from English to Finnish as he lost himself to the fury, the inconceivable consideration then realization that he was beaten.

Faz dropped and writhed on the floor, screaming in agony for the valiant fight he'd put up, even as Mithnite and Dancer emerged from their penance and lay gasping. They rose slowly, standing there next to useless as vampire fought vampire and I continued to take out those who broke through.

Faz calmed as his pain subsisted, then to my surprise he was on his feet.

"Got off lightly," he said as he came close, grinning.

"You back?" I asked, unable to contain my own smile.

"I'm back, baby, and the future looks bright."

We held hands and turned to smile at our son, standing behind us, an angry expression on his face for being left out of the fight. He saw us looking and came forward. Faz and I broke apart and each of us took one of Kane's hands and we faced down what remained of our foe.

The others joined us. Mithnite, Dancer, and Persimmon. We stood in a line, protected by a small band of vampires intent on change, and ready for action.

The fighting stopped, everyone exhausted, hardly anyone left who opposed us, and then the way parted and Oskari came forward, even those on our side shifting to allow him to approach.

"You think you've won?" he spat, eyes burning. "I'll kill you all. Don't you know who I am, what I can do?"

Something snapped, like I actually heard the twang as my body dug deep of the true power I held within. He'd messed with me and mine, tried to take everything from me, and for that I would see him dead. The Hidden magic I now owned like a second skin erupted inside, flooding my system with an energy and a lightness like secret whispers. It burst into my ink, so rapid that the skin split apart where it was at its thinnest.

Faz and Kane were thrown aside and I strode forward, my body burning, flesh and bone consumed not with hatred but a weariness over the whole damn thing. I looked down at myself and I was white, shining like a damn angel of death. Incandescent with sparks of dancing light that fizzled and burned the floor, my footsteps charring the rock itself.

Everyone moved away as I approached Oskari. As my aura grew more fierce, the inner strength of a mother scorned finally surfaced and I truly awoke to a power I hadn't known existed. This was why Kane was who he was, how he was such a person. I had given it to him, I had this all along and now it had manifest.

"The One," said the lead dwarf as he nodded, seemingly in approval, from the closing circle of dwarves and trolls.

"The One," they all repeated.

I looked around only to see nodding heads and confusion on the part of my friends and family, and then I understood what the dwarf had been telling me.

This wasn't about Kane, or Faz, or anyone else, this was about me and the future of my kind. About the future of vampire. With access to the Empty, something missing had finally been restored, something great and something dangerous and something I had to find for myself.

Vampires would know magic and they would cease their killing of innocents. Magic was ours if we wanted it, and it would help stem the terrible urges we felt, help control the craving for blood. We could take fuel and sustenance from the Empty. It would take time, it would hurt like hell, same as it did for all magic users, but there had to be a price to pay, there must be a cost for such a life, such a curse, as was right. We could exist, even thrive, but we must pay for our very existence with pain.

Somehow, everyone in the room understood this, and Oskari wasn't exempt. He knew what had happened, understood things could never be the same again. The old days were over, a new dawn was beginning, and, love it or loathe it, I was to lead this new age, at least in our country.

I was the Mother, I was the First, and I was to bear this terrible burden of change upon my shoulders. The One.

A small price to pay. I had my son; I had my husband; I had my humanity.

"You ready?" I asked Oskari, not unkindly.

"I am."

Oskari knelt, and so did everyone else. I stepped up to him, looked down with tears in my eyes, and I whispered, "Goodbye, Father."

I don't know if I was talking to him or someone long dead but still always in my head, or maybe just the past itself. But as I slammed out my rigid fingers and crushed Oskari's head, I put it all where it was meant to be, in the past.

Oskari slumped to the ground and I looked up, saw the truth of the future that awaited me, that awaited us all. It wasn't exactly pretty, but it was better than it had been, and at least we'd stand a chance.

The trolls moved as one, saying nothing. They just left, silent but for their footsteps. The dwarves weren't quite as hushed, were already telling tales that would grow ever more outlandish as they were repeated through the centuries. But this was where it all began, where a reluctant vampire enforcer first changed the course of history not just for vampires but for every Hidden species there had ever been or ever would be.

Me, I just wanted a cup of tea and a lie down. But that didn't happen.

The head dwarf, whoever he was, and maybe he was nobody special, same as me, took my hand. I was too stunned to resist, and with the others trailing, he led me away.

The Looking Room

Exhausted as we were, once we were taken to the Looking and Listening Room there was no way we could just leave when such a momentous change was occurring in the Hidden world. We watched for hours, Ward after Ward, House after House, country after country. Dwarves and trolls appeared from the gateways and fought against Hidden. Or in the case of the trolls simply walked through robust defenses, through buildings, through walls, and destroyed vampires on an epic scale.

It didn't end there though.

Local Heads, country Heads, even those on the World Council themselves, all became part of the final cleansing. The trolls led the action, with the dwarves doing most of the killing, as the large mass of the stoic watchers was more suited to squashing en masse than being selective about who to kill and who to spare.

People were eliminated without a reason given, others were told they were in charge without an explanation, but as bodies piled up and time passed and everyone communicated, it became clear this was happening for a reason. House cleaning Hidden style.

Nobody could stop it. There was nowhere to hide.

The trolls knew everything, where everyone was, where they hid, probably thanks to their own silent communications and the dwarves' strange rooms, which I suspected were more numerous than we'd been led to believe.

There was no warning, no quarter given, the trolls simply knew who was to be destroyed and who should be spared. Maybe they got it right, maybe they didn't, but there was no stopping them. High or low, powerful or just a novice or apprentice, nobody was exempt. Every human Hidden was a target, every mortal or ex-mortal that resided permanently on planet earth was judged, seemingly in an instant, yet I got the feeling they had been weighing us up since the beginning.

The trolls knew, and with the help of the dwarves they carried out a worldwide attack that began the instant I defeated Oskari and took upon myself the mantle of responsibility for my country and my kind. With our actions, we had made a choice for everyone. We gave the trolls the green light to put right so many wrongs and set human Hidden on a path that led not into darkness but hopefully into light.

Guess it had been a long time coming.

Life changed forever that day, and I knew I could never go back to how things were, no matter how much

I wanted to. But I had my husband, I had my son, and I had my friends.

And that was all I ever wanted from this life. Family.

The End.

Get new release notifications first via the Newsletter at alkline.co.uk.

Author's Note

Thanks for reading. I hope you enjoyed this, the third and last in the Hidden Blood series.

Kate's adventures begin directly after book 8 in the Dark Magic Enforcer series, although you do not need to read one to enjoy the other.

But if you do want to find out more about how we got where we currently are, learn how Kate and Faz got together, what happened on honeymoon, discover what Intus got up to that scarred everyone for life, and how Mithnite came to be their lodger, then please check out the Dark Magic Enforcer series.

Read about Faz's adventures, beginning with book 1: **Black Spark**, and trust me, it's a real blast. Literally.

Stay jiggy,

Al

19580741R00197

Printed in Poland
by Amazon Fulfillment
Poland Sp. z o.o., Wrocław